____RY PRESS

THE NAGA WARRIORS 1

Akshat Gupta belongs to a family of hoteliers and is now an established Bollywood screenwriter, poet and lyricist. He is a bilingual author and has been working on The Hidden Hindu trilogy for years. He was born in Chhattisgarh, grew up in Madhya Pradesh and now lives in Mumbai. You can connect with him on Instagram at @authorakshatgupta or send him an email on akshat.gupta0204@gmail.com.

From the bestselling author of **The Hidden Hindu** trilogy

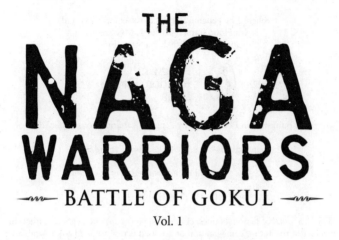

THE NAGA WARRIORS

BATTLE OF GOKUL

Vol. 1

AKSHAT GUPTA

EBURY
PRESS

An imprint of Penguin Random House

EBURY PRESS

Ebury Press is an imprint of the Penguin Random House group of companies
whose addresses can be found at global.penguinrandomhouse.com

Published by Penguin Random House India Pvt. Ltd
4th Floor, Capital Tower 1, MG Road,
Gurugram 122 002, Haryana, India

Penguin
Random House
India

First published in Ebury Press by Penguin Random House India 2024

Copyright © Bake My Cake Films Pvt Ltd 2024

ISBN 9780143465935

Typeset in Bembo Std by Manipal Technologies Limited, Manipal
Printed at Thomson Press India Ltd, New Delhi

www.penguin.co.in

Contents

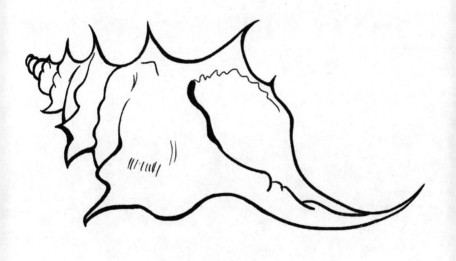

1

The Nameless Naga

In February 2024, a few days after the Ram temple in Ayodhya, Uttar Pradesh, was inaugurated, a middle-aged Naga sadhu walked barefoot on the high, vast and never-ending ranges of the Himalayas. The ascetic walked almost naked, in the serene silence of calm white mountains, wearing nothing but *rudraksh* bead necklaces and strings around his wrists and biceps, with his long dreadlocks. His chest and body were hairy and entirely smeared in sacred ash. His forehead bore a *tripoom* and his beard ran down to his chest.

Walking through the tough and bone chilling topography, the Naga noticed a set of fresh footprints in the mountain snow and realized that they were of a mountain hiker's. It was very rare to find another human being in the impossible terrain of the Himalayan peaks, so he followed the footsteps.

As he walked farther, he started finding hiking equipment scattered everywhere, almost buried in the snow.

A few steps ahead, he found many dead bodies. It seemed as if last night's avalanche had consumed them all. Out of all the bodies, one lay farther down, totally covered in thick snow, only a few fingers sticking out. As the Naga moved to the body to take a closer look, the fingers moved slightly. The body still had some life left in it!

The Naga dug the body out. It was a man. The hiker opened his eyes and they widened with fear at the sight of the wild-looking Naga sadhu, bare-bodied and barefoot, his face too close to the hiker's.

The hiker, too weak to do anything, fainted. When he came to his senses he realized that the Naga was dragging him by one of his legs towards a cave. He had heard stories about Aghoris and Naga sadhus being cannibals. He wanted to fight to defend himself but had no energy to even lift a finger. He accepted his fate and kept staring hopelessly at the open sky till it changed to the dark roof of the cave.

The darkness in the cave looked like death and he closed his eyes again. A few hours later, he woke up and saw the Naga sadhu sitting across him, a fire between them. The fire had never seemed so scary to him before. It felt like the fire of hell in which the Naga would burn him alive before eating him. He felt a little more strength in his muscles, so he begged for his life and said, 'Please don't kill me. Take whatever you need but spare my life.' The hiker knew that the Naga could not understand even a single word of his British English accent. The Naga stood up and walked to the hiker. The shadow he cast behind him on the uneven and rough walls of the cave was bigger than him and with the flames crackling in front of it, he looked like the demon of death, coming to swallow the hiker alive. The hiker started crawling away from the Naga despite knowing that there was absolutely no hiding or running, and no chance of any outside help.

The Naga sadhu came close to the hiker's face and opened his mouth. The hiker closed his eyes in fear, preparing to experience extreme pain when the Naga bit him.

'What's your name?' asked the Naga. The hiker slowly opened his eyes upon hearing the only language he knew and realized, to his surprise, that it was the wild Naga who was speaking English. It was a relief coming from a mouth he didn't expect to hear it from and in a place he never thought he would be.

'How do you speak my language?' asked the hiker, still cautious and nervous.

'I am a Naga sadhu, not an illiterate. I am saving your life, not killing you. Now! What's your name?' asked the Naga.

'I am Thomas Stones! Who are you?' replied the hiker, with a little confidence he had gained in the last few seconds.

'I am exactly who I look like, just not a cannibal. Do not fear me. Now get back to the fire. It's too cold for you outside. You need heat and food to regain your strength and recover.'

The hiker felt a little relief and silently agreed to whatever the Naga said as he realized that the Naga was right.

They both settled in front of each other, the fire between them.

Thomas suddenly said, 'I thought you would kill me . . . and . . .'

'And eat you? We don't do that. It is a myth,' replied the nameless Naga rightly predicting the second half of Thomas's statement.

'So you can survive without flesh?' asked Thomas, indirectly reconfirming his safety.

'We are not addicted to anything. At times we don't even need food for weeks, though we can eat anything that's available,' replied the Naga offering a food bowl to the hiker.

'Thank you for your generosity. I would have died out there. You saved me,' said the hungry hiker, picking up the bowl.

The Naga bowed in acceptance of the hiker's gratitude.

Breaking the ice between them further, the hiker continued, 'You already know my name, but let me reintroduce myself. I come from Canterbury, England, and I am a professional hiker. I started hiking when I was eighteen and didn't stop until today, when you saved me. What's your story?' asked Thomas.

The nameless Naga replied, 'I am a Naga and our clan's sole purpose is to protect dharma.'

'Naga? I had heard stories of Aghoris and Nagas before I decided to come to the Himalayas, but what I see now is something else. So, what is a Naga?' Thomas asked genuinely.

'To explain that I'll have to give you some background. Bharat was a land of great prosperity and wisdom for thousands of years. It boasted a thriving economy, driven by flourishing trade routes that connected it to the rest of the world. Bharat was renowned for its culture, natural beauty, advanced technology and science, spirituality, teachings and values. It was also famous for its bountiful resources, including valuable spices, textiles and precious gems that attracted traders from far and wide. This abundance of wealth facilitated the construction of splendid cities adorned with majestic temples and palaces and attracted many foreign invaders, looters and enemies of our dharma.

'Years and centuries passed thus. Our dharma needed an extraordinary scholar with superhuman spiritual capabilities and a prescient view of the centuries to come. A boy was born in 788 AD in a village named Kalandy, which is now a town not far from Cochin in Kerala. His parents were an aged, childless couple who led a devout life serving the poor. They named their child Shankara, which meant giver of prosperity.

'Son of Aryamba and Shivaguru, he was none other than Adi Guru Shankaracharya, a significant spiritual icon who enlightened Bharat with his teachings. After leaving his home in his early youth, he sought wisdom under the guidance of Govinda, mastering his learning on the tranquil shores of the Narmada River in Omkareshwar, in the sacred city of Varanasi along the Ganges and surrounded by the majestic Himalayas in Badrinath. Shankaracharya emerged not only as an exceptional intellect and genius in linguistic skills but also as a spiritual beacon, embodying the pride of Bharat and offering timeless wisdom that continues to inspire humanity. Shankaracharya left his body and this world at the young age of thirty-two. But before his demise, he organized the Hindu monks from ten sects into four Mathas with four headquarters: Jagannatha Puri in the east, Dwarka in the west, Badrikashrama in the north and Sringeri in the south. Each Matha was headed by one of his four main disciples. He knew that in the centuries to come, dharma would face threats and along with wisdom, it would require warriors and weapons to survive. He foresaw that besides the spirituality and knowledge of sadhus, dharma would need soldiers to defend it and fight. What he created was a corps of sadhu soldiers who had wisdom in one hand and weapons in the other. These sadhus were named Naga sadhus, and I am one of them.

'Scholars in ancient Bharat were pioneers in various fields, including mathematics, astronomy, medicine and philosophy. The invention of the decimal numeral system, which included the concept of zero, originated in Bharat, shaping the future of mathematics. Astronomers made precise observations of the sky and stars, while the Ayurvedic system of medicine laid the foundation for medical advancements.

'As Bharat flourished, it became a hub of intellectual activity. Prestigious centres of learning like Nalanda and Taxila attracted scholars from around the world. These institutions nurtured the growth of diverse branches of knowledge, from profound philosophy to intricate linguistics and rich literature.

'However, this age of prosperity and enlightenment was under threat. Invaders began to disrupt the peace, wreaking havoc on India's rich culture and dharma. Countless Hindu people fell victim to the invaders' ruthless campaigns, resulting in the destruction of temples and scriptures and the suppression of knowledge.

'This was the time for which Adi Guru Shankaracharya conceptualized the Naga warrior corps, ascetics who would serve as guardians of the faith and protectors of dharma.

'The main aim of the Naga sadhu corps created by Adi Guru Shankaracharya was clear: to safeguard the rich spiritual and philosophical traditions of Bharat. They were entrusted with the duty of defending temples, sacred scriptures and spiritual knowledge from external threats.

'Adi Shankaracharya's creation of the Naga warriors was a response to the turbulent times when Bharat's wealth and knowledge were under siege. These ascetic guardians became a symbol of resilience, preserving the nation's spiritual and intellectual heritage despite the challenges that invaders posed. Their legacy endures as a testament to Bharat's glorious past and its unwavering commitment to protecting its riches and knowledge. Adi Shankaracharya wanted to send a message to the people of Bharat—that they would have to use education and weapons together to save their dharma when attacked.

'Later, the Nagas, whom Shankaracharya had trained, dispersed and went all over Bharat to spread awareness of the power of knowledge, the importance of protecting it and the art of war.

'Adi Guru Shankaracharya died in the year 820 A.D. in Kedarnath but the war with the enemies of our faith is still on even today. We need to fight.'

'Which era are you living in, sadhu? You are no soldier and there is no war going on. It's February 2024,' said Thomas.

'It is still on. There is peace now because we fought wars. A war that started around 650 years ago and is still on.'

'Still on? What do you mean? Which war are you talking about?'

2

The First Blood

The magical world of Bharat, which had rejoiced at the names of the Gods for centuries, was now suffering as the Mughals and the Mongols came to scratch and bleed it. Kingdoms fought among themselves, allowing the intruders to settle there, lured by gold. The invaders destroyed the temples, looted the land and enforced their beliefs upon the natives.

The Hindus believed that they had seen every type of suffering life had to offer; little did they know that the worst was yet to come. The worst, most unimaginable horrors were delivered to them by a man named Ahmad Shah Abdali. When there was a decline in the power of the Mughals in northern and central Bharat, and the Maratha warriors were emerging to expand their Maratha empire, heralded by their cries of 'Har Har Mahadev', in Delhi, the leading ulema, Shah Waliullah, was shaken to his core at the prospect of a non-Muslim rising to power. Scared, he penned nine letters and sent them to the king of the Afghans, whose full name was Ahmad Shah Abdali Dur-e-Durran, one of the most ruthless and merciless invaders that history had ever documented. The letters said, 'If you don't come to Bharat, defending us from the Marathas, history will treat you as a coward and a traitor and your lineage will never hear the call of azan.' These lines gave Abdali his next mission: to advance into central India and save his unborn lineage. Towering, with a massive and heavily muscular body, he had menacing eyes and an intimidating aura. His name was a symbol of terror and torture. It was rumoured that every path his armies took bore the stench of death for months. Flying green flags and armed with the best weapons of his time, he started raiding Hindu villages and brutally ripped apart the rich silk tapestry of Bharat.

Peshawar was a convenient point for Abdali and his army to enter Bharat. He first crossed the Indus River in 1748 and conquered Lahore.

The nameless Naga continued: It was the winter of 1749. The evening air was crisp and chilly as the sun was setting, painting the sky in hues of bright pink and orange. At the edge of a plain on one of the Vindhya ranges of central Bharat, a group of horsemen were staring at the lush green land far below when their gaze stopped on a small settlement in the lap of the valley. The soft glow of lights flickered from afar like a million fireflies in a small bush. The atmosphere in Village Bichhiya was alive with the spirit of Diwali.

As per the ancient, traditional practice, the entrance of each hut was decorated with vibrant rangolis that the young girls and women of the household had spent hours preparing. Each rangoli was a piece of art. The grand mandala and floral designs, outlined in rice flour and filled with a variety of dry colours, flower petals and turmeric, were made fresh to welcome the goddess of wealth, luck and prosperity, Goddess Lakshmi.

The villagers were dressed in their finest that night. Men wore white cotton dhotis and the women were adorned in radiant *cholis* and saris, necklaces made of pearls and gold beads around their necks, colourful golden and silver bangles on their wrists and more than half a dozen white bamboo combs decorating their heads. Their happiness was infectious, their laughter more dazzling than the ornaments they wore.

Amid this celebration, the village temple stood tall. A symbol of their faith and collective identity, its grandeur was a reflection of the prosperity and cultural richness of the village.

In Hindu culture, in those days, a temple was much more than a place of worship. It was not just a symbol of faith but also of hope, a place where children learnt about the history, culture, beliefs along with science of that time and significance of gods and goddesses. A place where gods were believed to descend upon earth to bless newly married couples. It was a site to perform sacred rituals, hold processions to ward off negative forces and offer flowers and prasad to deities as gratitude for the gift of life. It was a place of pilgrimage, known as *tirtha*, and the main aim of a temple was to inculcate an understanding of dharma (virtues of an ethical life) and *moksha* (self-realization and self-knowledge) through Bhakti yoga (devotion).

The villagers gathered in the courtyard of the temple, their hearts filled with faith, their eyes alight with immense devotion. They were there to offer their prayers, their gratitude to the divine for the year gone by and to seek blessings for the year to come.

Little children and elders alike admired the walls of the temple, which were covered in intricate carvings depicting stories from the rich history of Hindus; their complexity a demonstration of the skill of their creators.

Inside the temple, the air was heavy with the scent of fire and flowers, the atmosphere reverberating with the hum of prayers and chants. Lining the walls of the temple were statues of gods and goddesses. Lord Rama with his mighty bow, Maa Sita standing strong beside him and Hanuman kneeling before them, all felt entirely real. Another statue was of Krishna playing his flute with his mesmerizing, spell-binding smile, symbolizing eternal love. The other equally mesmerizing statue was of Goddess Durga with ten hands seated on a lion, each of her hands representing the characteristics of human behaviour that every person should possess. The ten arms of Goddess Durga held a sword, a *trishul* (trident), a mace, a *chakra* (discus), a bow and an arrow, a conch, a lotus, a thunderbolt, a snake and a flame to protect Her devotees from all directions, namely the eight corners, the sky and the earth.

The idol of Goddess Kaali was adorned with a necklace of demon heads and a skirt made of hands. She was dark and had red eyes, her tongue protruded from her mouth and her body was smeared with blood. Her four arms held a sword, the head of a demon, a vessel to collect the dripping blood and a trident.

Seated on a lotus wearing a red sari with golden threads and bedecked with gold, Goddess Lakshmi showcased her beauty and grace, depicting the true meaning of infinite beauty. Her four hands held wealth and prosperity, gold, coins and a lotus. Each figure was exquisitely carved, the expressions capturing myriad divine sentiments. These statues were covered in gold and studded with precious jewels, reflecting the wealth and devotion of the villagers.

As the group of horsemen atop the mountain observed this village, a large army slowly gathered behind them.

In the courtyard of the temple, a group of children was engrossed in its own celebrations, creating small structures made of stones. The air was filled with their giggles and cheerful banter as they competed to build the highest tower. Suddenly, a tower of stones tumbled down, bringing a young boy's hard work crashing to the ground. Tears welled up in the boy's eyes and started to roll down his cheeks.

The boy's father, who was observing from a distance, rushed to his side. Kneeling, he gently asked, 'What happened, my son?' Through his sobs, the boy explained his frustration, his effort gone in vain.

'Mine was the tallest and the best tower, *baba*! But I failed,' he cried.

The father silently comforted his son and then said, 'The Gita teaches us that if you continue to work hard and do your best, leaving the outcome to God, you'll find peace. God, the eternal unity, keeps balance and peace in the universe. This is simply a test he has set up for you. He wants to see if you make it again or give up. I suggest you start all over again and the gods will smile upon you with their blessings. He wants you to learn that life will always test you, but the one who stands up and starts again will eventually succeed in seeking the gods. He is teaching you that falling is not a mistake, but not standing back up and trying again is. Falling and failing may not be solely in your hands, my son, but getting back on your feet and trying harder again is, and that is exactly what our gods always test.'

The boy's eyes shimmered with newfound understanding and he flashed a bright smile. However, the moment of understanding was shattered as the ground beneath them started shaking. One by one, all the stone towers that the other children had built so diligently started falling to the ground. Alarmed by this sudden trembling, the father held on to his son tightly as parents rushed to their children and gathered family members together. Soon, screams and shouts erupted from outside the temple.

The screams of women and the howls of death signalled the arrival of the armed invaders. They charged into the village like a vicious storm. Dressed in layers of rough, dark leather and iron plate armour, wearing black turbans, their faces dripping brutality, eyes devoid of mercy, their souls hungry for blood, they looked like vengeful asuras who had returned to this holy land. Their swords, curved and wickedly sharp, glowed with a malicious darkness. The villagers knew them as Afghan soldiers.

Before anyone could react, the invaders were among them. Huts were set ablaze using the diyas placed outside their doors; the thatched roofs, made of straw and hay, caught fire quickly, turning the cheerful Diwali lights into a horrifying hellfire. Men were cut down mercilessly and their pleas for mercy were drowned by the invaders' savage war cries. Blood started to pool in the dusty lanes, the horrifying scent of it filling the air. Children's cries punctuated the air, terror etched on their innocent faces.

The women's festive clothes, now stained with dust and blood, were stripped off even as they tried to protect themselves and their daughters. Their screams echoed through the village, a haunting soundtrack to the horrifying scene. The bodies of men, young and old alike, lay scattered around like discarded dolls. It was tough to identify which body part belonged to which dead men, a heart-wrenching testimony to the ruthless onslaught.

As the Naga narrated the story, the hiker closed his eyes in dismay. His face conveyed the pain he felt. 'You are hurt listening to this? Imagine those who lived it,' said the nameless Naga and continued his tale.

In no time, the men were dead, the children were tied up and caged, and girls and women stood nude. The Afghan men surrounding them were freely choosing the terror-stricken females for their one-night leisure and the women wanted to reach for weapons to kill themselves.

One of the middle-aged women broke through the circle of soldiers and ran out towards her own burning house. Two men chased her thinking she was trying to escape but before they could lay their filthy hands on her, she jumped into the fire. She chose to die before the rape, but not all the others were that lucky. They had to go through an unimaginable, painful and shameful process before they were consigned to death.

In the middle of all of this chaos, some soldiers barged into the temple. It was now time to strip the gods and goddesses of their gold, jewels and silk clothes. The divine figures, once radiant, now stood desecrated and bare. But the invaders' hunger for sacrilege was not yet satiated. The soldiers started breaking the statues one by one. First, they pulled apart the goddesses, flinging the bare statues to the ground and stomping on them with their feet till all their arms broke. One of the soldiers pulled the bow away from Lord Rama's statue and then used it to poke and prod Rama and Sita's statues till they fell. He then hammered them till they disintegrated into rubble. The same was the fate of the statues of Krishna. A war that started then is still on. Temples are still broken in ancient Bharat that is called Pakistan and Bangladesh for the time being, before we claim it back.

The Naga took a pause and continued narrating the past again. When they entered the Shiva temple, the man commanding the unit sat on the Nandi idol placed right in front of the Shiva linga. His right eye was smaller than the other, he wore clothes in green and black and a thick, long beard extended from his chin, with no moustache above his lips. His soldiers held a few Hindu men and women by their hair while a solider ran from his side and dealt a blow to the Shiva linga, breaking it into pieces. To further humiliate the priest of the temple and the other prisoners, the commander got down from Nandi's statue and pissed on the shattered pieces of statues scattered all around. The commander laughed his loudest: 'My name is Mujib. That means God and from now on, I am your God. Kneel before me.' The soldiers began to laugh along with their commander. The Hindu priest could no longer bear the humiliation of his gods and refused to go on his knees. He exclaimed in anger, 'Pray to your gods, for I am sure that one day, riding on his Nandi, Lord Shiva will come to remind you of this night.' Mujib walked to the priest and slashed his head off with a sword. The boy stood near his father's dead body and watched it all, waiting for his gods to end his test.

In the final act of devastation, they set the temple ablaze, after collecting all the precious stones and ornaments from the statues. The sacred temple, which minutes ago had echoed with prayers, now echoed with the crackling of fire and the desecration of sanctity. The village, once a vibrant canvas of celebration, was now a horrifying spectacle of brutality and devastation. It was a chilling sight of genocide that transformed the serene night into a terrifying spectacle of destruction and despair. The kids were taken for circumcision (*dharma parivartan*) and the women to reproduce illegitimate children by force to add to the army of darkness and asuras for the times to come.

This continued for years. It was the year 1757 when Abdali's blood-soaked feet stained the sacred temples of Kashi and Mathura, leaving behind trails of Hindu dead bodies. First, he separated the men, women and children. The men would be beheaded one by one in front of their families or burnt and buried alive. Each and every girl and woman was dragged out of her house, stripped in front of her children and raped in the open. They weren't just torturing innocent people, they did it with the intent of breaking their spirits completely, destroying their belief in their Gods. Boys were circumcised and converted.

During that time, two Naga sadhus were wandering on foot. Their ash-covered gray bodies stood out starkly against the everyday colours of life. Their hair was a wild jumble of dreadlocks, adorned with the rustic brown rudraksh beads. Their kohl-lined fiery eyes reflected their intense devotion. Strips of cloth hung loosely around their waists, a lone concession to the modesty of the material world. Upon noticing smoke and fire rising in the distance from Kashi, they ventured into the city. The scene that welcomed them was devastating. They scoured the holy places, desperately seeking survivors, but found none. They saw the temple flags lying on the ground, disrespected and cast aside. The sight was gut-wrenching even for the Nagas and the shock was evident in their eyes.

'What should we do? How did this happen?' exclaimed one of them.

'We must leave for the matha at once,' replied the other sadhu as he picked up a flag, wrapped it around his forehead, tied another to his stick and raised it skyward. They immediately began their journey to the matha, one of the religious orders established by Adi Shankaracharya as a centre of learning and spiritual guidance.

A few other Naga sadhus in Ujjain and Mathura had also been witness to similar scenes of carnage. To report what they had witnessed, these Nagas also rushed to the matha.

Heading towards the matha from various directions, the Nagas travelled across mountain ranges, crossed rivers and traversed through villages. It took them nine days to reach the matha, looking for the Mathadhish. A small crowd gathered around them as they frantically ran through the streets looking for their guru. As they got closer to the ashram, their pace also quickened. 'Mathadhish, we request an audience,' they shouted.

The Mathadhish stepped out of the ashram. Finally, the Naga sadhus were standing in front of the Mathadhish.

The Mathadhish was an old man in his late sixties. The wrinkles on his face and the serenity in his eyes spoke of his wisdom, age and experience. He had long white dreadlocks flowing down all the way to his feet, which were in contrast to his tanned and weathered skin covered in ash.

Accounts of the Afghani raids, mass massacres and horrific acts committed on the villagers, bottled up in the sadhus' hearts throughout the days of travel, were ready to burst like an explosion from a volcano.

'Bodies of the dead . . . blood of the innocents everywhere . . . fire of darkness and smoke of fear . . . burnt men . . . naked women . . . mutilated children. . . shattered idols and statues . . . demolished temples . . . our dharma is in danger . . .' The Naga sadhus could barely get full sentences out as their eyes filled with the memories of the ghastly visuals.

Looking deep in their eyes, the Mathadhish ordered in his deep and heavy voice, 'Silence!'

As they looked back into the Mathadhish's eyes, all of them were hypnotized into a calm trance. They sat down quietly on the ground as they were unable to keep their eyes open, their breathing visibly slow. The Mathadhish continued looking deep into their eyes. He was really hypnotizing them. It was like when doctors administer sedative injections to calm your nerves, slow your heartbeat and make you fall asleep for your well-being. 'Now sleep and do not wake up till you hear "Har Har Mahadev",' instructed the Mathadhish. The tired and agitated Naga sadhus immediately fell asleep, hypnotized.

Upon hearing the disturbing news, the Mathadhish was concerned. He ordered: 'All sadhus and *sadhvis* should gather at Gokul on the night of Shukla paksha, twenty-one days hence.'

The Mathadhish turned towards a few Naga men who were waiting for their next orders and said with a heaviness in his voice, 'Find Ajaa and Shambhu.'

'Ajaa and Shambhu? Who are they?' Thomas, the hiker asked. The nameless Naga looked into the distance for a moment, as if gathering his thoughts and then spoke with the utmost respect and warmth.

3

Ajaa and Shambhu Ji

The nameless Naga started answering Thomas's question. Ajaa was an intrinsic part of Shambhu ji. Together, Ajaa and Shambhu ji were a unique amalgamation of faith and strength. If Shambhu ji was fire, Ajaa was his flame, if Shambhu ji was rain, Ajaa was his thunder, if Ajaa was the light, Shambhu ji was the source, if Shambhu ji was the sword, Ajaa was the blade. Ajaa was Shambhu ji's creation, his life's work and also his most compelling work of war. Early morning the next day, a few Nagas were all set to embark upon a journey to find Ajaa and Shambhu ji. They only knew Ajaa and Shambhu ji had been travelling south but had no information other than that.

'Look for the symbols of Shiva, the deity you so embody, on the walls of temples and homes, and on the bark of the trees. These marks will be your guiding light and will lead you to Ajaa and Shambhu,' instructed the Mathadhish.

The Nagas now knew how to find them. They travelled for days, climbing mountains, crossing rivers, passing through several towns and hiking through treacherous forests in search of Ajaa and Shambhu ji. Finally, two Nagas, Dinanath, a middle-aged Naga who recognized Ajaa's face, and Adhiraj, a comparatively younger Naga who always carried a *shankh* with him, tied to his waist, reached a dead end on the shore of a huge lake at the bottom of a waterfall named Mahendi Kund, which was so high that it felt like the water was falling from the skies.

'Shankh? What is that?' asked the hiker. A shankh is a conch shell and is of spiritual significance in Hindu tradition as it is believed to usher in auspicious beginnings and ward off evil, explained the nameless Naga.

Dinanath and Adhiraj stood near the bottom of the waterfall wondering how to move ahead. Trying to assess the strength they would need to reach the top of the waterfall, both of them looked at the peak of the waterfall. As they squinted to get a good look at the top, their eyes landed on a man who was sitting calmly and meditating.

Perched atop a gigantic boulder, he sat in the middle of a roaring waterfall. His meditating shadow fell on the rock. The rays of the setting sun fell on his bare back, painting him in gold. His faint reflection was cast on the flowing water.

His body was a testament to his strength. His forearms were tight and corded. Veins popped from the wrists and biceps. He had sharp, long nails. He wore nothing but sacred strings of white thread, the *janeyu*, also called the *upanayana*. It was a symbol of spirituality and sacrifice and showed that a guru had accepted the individual under his guidance as his *shishya* (student). Strings of rudraksh beads were wrapped around his neck and wrists. There was a coat of ash all over his chest. A messy bun of long dreadlocks crowned his head, a symbol of his spiritual path. A tripoorn of sandalwood was drawn on his forehead and between it was a *tilak*.'

'Tripoorn? Tilak? What does that signify?' asked the curious hiker with his eyes glued to the nameless Naga as he waited for a reply.

The tripoorn is a spiritual symbol in the tradition of Lord Shiva, which consists of three horizontal lines and a red tilak in the centre. The lines are made with sacred ash (from the remains of the sacred fire) or with sandalwood, and it is usually drawn on the forehead. It is believed that whoever bears this symbol on their body is cleansed of all sins irrespective of whether they follow any other virtues or understand them. The three lines are said to be the representation of the three intentions of man, namely, Kriya Shakti (power of work), Ichha Shakti (power of will) and Gyana Shakti (power of knowledge). Life is defined in three stages created by God: creation, sustenance and destruction. The tilak in the centre represents the unity of energy and matter, and that mankind has to go through all the three stages. It is said that after a person applies a tripoorn, all the accumulated sins of their current and past lives can be removed, the nameless Naga answered the hiker, whose eyes now showed an eagerness to know more about the man the nameless Naga was describing.

Water thrashed down all around him, spraying him with droplets that twinkled like diamonds in the sunlight just for a moment and then evaporated immediately. Smoke rose from his entire body. The mist created by the waterfall enveloped him, adding a mystical aura around the man. Amid the thunderous roar of the waterfall and the serene radiance of the sun, he was meditating, a beacon of tranquillity and hope. His eyes were shut calmly in a trance. As the sun's rays illuminated his figure, he seemed to be an embodiment of Lord Shiva himself.

Positioned beneath the tremendous heights of this majestic waterfall, gazing upon this spectacle, the two Naga sadhus were rapt with awe, their eyes fixed on the meditating man. Watching the man from afar, the Naga sadhus' eyes filled with devotion as they realized that their search had ended. The meditating man with the janeyu, the tripoorn and the tilak was Ajaa.

'Ajaa . . . blazing like gold,
calm like silver,
resilient like iron,
and sharp like a sword.
Sight of an eagle,
strength of a bull.
Like the pyre he burns,
yet is cool like the ashes of a sacred fire.
The balance of trishul and *trinetra*.
Still like a mountain
when his eyes are closed,

volatile like an earthquake
when his eyes opened.
Look at him with love and you'll see an innocent child
inside him. Look at him with anger and you'll awaken
the beast within.'

The nameless Naga continued his saga. While the sadhus
wondered how to reach Ajaa, a magnificent peacock took
flight from right in front of them, gliding up to join its flock
outside a temple placed at the zenith of a small mountain
nearby, with bells strung all around the temple's *mandapa*.
Embracing this divine clue, Dinanath laboriously climbed
up the mountain till he reached the mandapa.

After catching his breath, he started ringing the temple
bells with both hands and his voice rose in chants of 'Har
Har Mahadev!' Adhiraj began blowing into the shankh,
producing the ॐ sound, a sacred and transformative
vibration.

The atmosphere was thick with the echoes of the bells
and the transcendent sound of the shankh. It felt as though
they were sounding a call to war. The mighty chants of 'Har
Har Mahadev', the piercing sound of the shankh and the
resounding gong of the bells created a powerful symphony,
stirring up a sense of anticipation, courage and faith that
seemed to merge with the rhythmic roar of the waterfall,
and echoed off the mountain walls to reach Ajaa.

The moment the rousing sounds reached Ajaa, his eyes
flickered open. Dark brown, deep-set eyes, they radiated
a certain intensity. He turned his gaze towards the Naga

sadhus who stood with folded hands. As he rose to his feet, each muscle in his body flexed and glistened under the setting sun.

'Without a moment of hesitation, Ajaa launched himself off the rock, diving straight into the waterfall. The sight of his dive left Adhiraj astounded. He stared at the spot on the waterfall where he had disappeared. Minutes passed by with no sign of Ajaa and the sadhus hurried back to the shore of the lake, their hearts pounding with concern.

Just when a wave of worry started to ripple among them, Ajaa emerged from the lake's depths. Water streamed down his long, open hair like Ganga. Ajaa grabbed his long hair and started to tie it. Adhiraj was awestruck by the mighty Ajaa as the crescent moon was placed right above his head, making him appear even more like Lord Shiva. The crescent moon looked like it was tied to his hair and his resurfacing was akin to Lord Shiva himself descending from Kailash Parbat.

The Naga sadhus greeted Ajaa. With a respectful bow of his head, Ajaa reciprocated . His dark brown eyes, full of depth and intensity, moved attentively over each face before him, one that he knew and the other, with the shankh, that he didn't. His gaze was unflinching, piercing through the apparent calm and identifying the worry etched subtly on Adhiraj's face.

Dinanath began to narrate the events that had transpired: 'Upon hearing the disturbing news, the Mathadhish ordered us to summon you. He commanded that all sadhus and sadhvis should gather in Gokul on the night of Shukla paksha.'

Dinanath's eyes flickered with an urgent flame as he added, 'We need to leave for Gokul. Now!' The sadhu's words cut through the air, carrying with them a heavy sense of urgency.

'Shambhu ji? asked Ajaa.

'The other Naga sadhus are searching for him,' replied Adhiraj, tying his shankh back on his waist.

The other Naga sadhus, in their quest for Shambhu ji, had reached an old town named Maheshwar, which was situated 50 kilometres south of the Mahendi Kund waterfall and which lay on the north bank of the Narmada River in Madhya Pradesh. On the outskirts of this historic town was a *gurukul*, the most well-known system of imparting education to children. Surrounded by forests, the gurukul was a collection of small huts made of bamboo, mud and thatch, perfectly in harmony with nature. There was a huge, open courtyard with a large tree in the centre where the children would gather for their morning prayers. The courtyard also had a fire altar where y*ajnas* would be lit for various ceremonies. Classes were conducted inside the small huts or under the shade of the trees. The gurukul was a symbol of discipline and devotion where, at the termination of one's education, each student had to present their guru with a *gurudakshina*. The gurukul was more than just a place of learning; it was a holistic environment where students learnt to live in harmony with nature and imbibed values that would last them a lifetime.

A fifty-four-year-old Naga sadhu was sneaking around the pathways of the gurukul. He had a serious face lined with wrinkles, but his eyes sparkled with a mischievous light, a hint of his playful nature. A warm spirit resided in his hard outer shell, much like a sweet kernel hiding inside a tough nut.

His rolling walk was artless and he was unselfconscious, like Hanuman, one of the avatars of Lord Shiva. He roamed around the grounds of the gurukul with a light, playful step, as if he were playing a silent game of hide-and-seek. As he passed a small hut he stopped, noticing it full of little boys and girls waiting for their teacher to arrive.

The girls were dressed in colourful lehengas and cute little blouses, while the boys wore dhotis and kurtas.

Their collective silence niggled at his playful side and their innocent and disciplined behaviour drew the old man in.

Their faces were bright and curious, and they sat in quiet discipline. Entering the classroom with a fresh burst of energy, Shambhu ji, with a twinkle in his eyes, gazed at this bunch of cute, little young minds. The blackboard displayed the Hindi alphabets:

क से कलम, Ka for *kalam* (pen),
ख से खरबूजा, Kh for *kharbooja* (melon),
ग से गधा, Ga for *gadha* (donkey),
घ से घोड़ा, Gh for *ghoda* (horse)

With a sheepish grin, the old man wiped the Hindi words written next to the alphabets and replaced them with the most suited words.

क से काली माँ, Ka for Kaali Maa (Goddess Kaali)

ख से खड्ग, Kh for *khadag* (sword)

ग से गदा, Ga for *gadaa* (mace)

च से Gh for *ghuspaithiye* (invader)

The old Naga sadhu turned to the children with the chalk in his hand. Due to the old man's appearance, there was apprehension on the young faces and their eyes were wide with curiosity. 'Fear not,' said the old Naga, his voice firm yet soothing. 'We are going to learn a new lesson today.'

Brimming with energy, the old man started teaching the new words, bringing each to life with animated actions. 'Ka se Kaali.' He widened his eyes and pulled his tongue out quickly, imitating the fearsome Goddess Kaali. The children could no longer contain their excitement, their previous silence giving way to giggles and laughter. The old man joined the excited children and asked them to repeat the words after him.

Next, he pretended to swing a sword, showing 'Kh se khadag', the crescent moon-shaped double-edged sword of Goddess Kaali. The kids yelled and clapped in excitement, copying him by swinging their own pretend swords through the air.

When he got to 'Ga se gadaa', he puffed out his cheeks, widened his stance and mimicked the iconic pose of Lord Hanuman by holding the gadaa on his shoulders and said, 'Jai Siya Ram.' His playful mimicry drew a wave of laughter from the children, their high-pitched giggles ringing throughout the classroom as they imitated his actions with their tiny, enthusiastic gestures and said collectively, 'Jai Siya Ram.' The old man's stern exterior had transformed into a wellspring of energy and joy, revealing the warmth and humour hidden beneath.

Dhruv, the class teacher, heard the noise coming from his classroom. He watched the spectacle unfold and his brows furrowed in disapproval as he saw his class being disrupted by an unexpected, strange-looking old man. He marched towards the classroom, determined to confront the intruder.

Dhruv approached the stranger, visibly annoyed yet intrigued.

'Who are you to barge into my classroom and teach these kids these . . . these strange words? There is a syllabus we follow here and we teach accordingly,' said Dhruv, setting up the authority straight.

With a soft smile and in a gentle yet firm voice, the old man replied, 'I am just a Shiva devotee. Your name is Dhruv, right?' Dhruv, who was in his thirties and who wore a traditional attire of *janeyu* and dhoti, was a bit taken aback but the glitter in his eyes hinted at the wisdom far beyond the men of his age. However, creating such disorder on the regimented grounds of the gurukul was unacceptable to Dhruv.

'Here, we teach children about peace, about growth through the knowledge of the Vedas and the shastras, not about war,' exclaimed Dhruv.

The old man replied with the same gentleness, 'I respect your position as the class teacher. But you also seem too young. May I ask how old you are?'

'I am thirty-six, and I have dedicated my entire life to the education of these young children. I have much more experience in this field than you can imagine,' said Dhruv, visibly frustrated and offended.

The old man sighed, 'I have no doubt about your experience and intentions. Peace is precious, Dhruv, but along with it these children need to learn how to protect and preserve peace and for that, they must know that a protector and a preserver sometimes needs weapons to save peace and preserve our culture, our dharma and our rich scriptures.'

'Defence? By teaching them names of weapons?' exclaimed Dhruv.

The old man nodded. 'Yes, defence. Defence against those who come to bury us and our dharma. To uproot us from our land and our traditions.'

'Defending and protecting against whom? People like you bring chaos and violence into the world, conjuring imaginary threats. There's no need to protect as there is no threat out there. Don't kill the innocence of these kids by manipulating them and introducing them to terror.' Dhruv sharpened his tone and so did the old man.

'Dead innocence is still better than dead children. Closing your eyes will create darkness just for you, it will not turn the day into night. They have the right to weapons and its use and knowledge so that they can defend themselves if need be. There is a difference of night and day between terrorizing and training. There has been a threat to our dharma for hundreds of years. We all know what our dharma has to give in terms of knowledge and treasures. You know as well as I do the value of a balanced education. I do not propose we abandon the Vedas or the shastras. Instead, we add to that the knowledge of defence, the understanding of resilience,' replied the old man, maintaining his composure.

He continued, 'Don't be blind. A blind man can never prepare a visionary. Don't be blind to your ignorance. It is not violence we seek. It is protection and preservation. You teach them of our past, but if you will not prepare them for the sour present then there will be no future. Let me teach them of our present, our survival. *Shastra* (weapon) is as important as *shaastra* (wisdom). You teach them wisdom of the past and let me teach them weapons of the present. Together, we can secure their future.'

The old man looked into Dhruv's eyes. 'What are you afraid of? You are the successor of Parashuram . . . are you afraid that if you pick up an axe, you will never be able to put it down?'

Interrupting the intense debate between the old man and Dhruv, the two Naga men approached, calling the old man's name, 'Shambhu ji.' The old man turned, and the Nagas bowed and greeted him.

Dhruv looked at the respectful greeting and heard the name of Shambhu ji, the old man. He had received the answer to his question.

'Bam Bam Bhole,' the Nagas greeted him.

'Bam Bam Bhole! Is everything all right?' asked Shambhu ji, changing his tone firmly as he sensed their anxiety. Dhruv gauged Shambhu ji's importance and position from the shift in Shambhu ji's manner and the respect he commanded.

'We must leave for Gokul immediately. The Mathadhish has summoned you, Ajaa and all Naga sadhus to gather by Shukla paksha,' replied the two Nagas.

Dhruv overheard the conversation. However, not wanting to intrude, he picked up a piece of wet cloth and started erasing the text on the blackboard that Shambhu ji had written. As he erased the word *ghuspaithiye*, meaning invaders, Shambhu ji said, 'The invaders won't disappear by erasing just the word on a board. You too need to lift your weapon to erase them in real life. Think about it when you have time!'

With these parting words, Shambhu ji looked at the children once again, and stuck his tongue out and emitted an intimidating sound. In response, the classroom echoed with shouts of 'Ka se Kaali Maa'. He then mimicked Hanuman, prompting the kids to chant, 'Ga se gadaa.'

'Never forget that even our gods needed weapons at times of wars brought upon them by asuras. We all are children of gods, how can we think that we won't need them?' said Shambhu ji looking at the students but messaging Dhruv. As Shambhu ji walked away with the Naga men, he left behind a classroom filled with excitement and curiosity.

'Where is Ajaa?' asked Shambhu ji as he hurried away with the other Nagas.

'Ajaa is on his way to Gokul,' replied a Naga. Shambhu ji smiled and felt a wave of emotion at the prospect of reuniting with Ajaa.

Ajaa was on his arduous journey to Gokul while Shambhu ji was closing the distance from another direction. As they continued their journeys, they covertly spread the word about the gathering in Gokul to as many Nagas as possible in the villages along their way.

No one knew much about Ajaa's origin except that he had been orphaned at a young age, and that Shambhu ji had taken up the responsibility of training him to create a living lethal weapon, the most powerful Naga warrior.

Even in the urgency of reaching Gokul, Ajaa's eyes constantly searched for his guru, Shambhu ji.

4

The Disloyal Royal

The Afghans believed that, when it came to strength and viciousness, only one name echoed alongside Abdali's: Sardar Khan. It was rumoured that he had the strength of ten horses and attacked his enemies with the ferocity of a hundred hungry crocodiles. It was a hot day and the sun was upon their heads. The fabric of the grand tent rustled as Ahmad Shah Abdali's commander-in-chief, Sardar Khan, made his way towards Jugal Kishore, one of Abdali's major strategists. Sardar Khan was an intimidatingly tall man with an enormous build. His scarred face and towering personality would send chills down the spine of any man who stood against him. His turban sat heavily on his brow, symbolizing his high rank, and his attire was ornate and imposing.

Although Jugal Kishore was not as physically imposing as Sardar, he possessed an immense air of quiet power and eyes that sparkled with intelligence. A slight smile never entirely left his lips, and he seemed more like a chess master than a military strategist.

Inside the spacious tent that functioned as a makeshift war room, Sardar Khan laid down his plans to overthrow the Hindu kingdoms of Vijaygarh and Haripur. The maps spread out over a large table with miniature stone markers representing troops, animals and artillery, created a grand scene of power and strength.

'Jugal, we need a force of 8000 men, 500 horses, fifty cannons and 250 camels minimum,' Sardar Khan demanded, his voice booming inside the tent.

Jugal smirked, appearing casual.

'Jugal Kishore ji!' said Jugal.

'What?' Sardar Khan asked in confusion.

'Jugal Kishore *ji*!' Jugal repeated.

Sardar tried to stay calm, but his expressions revealed his frustration as he bit his tongue and repeated, 'Give me 8000 men, 500 horses, fifty cannons and 250 camels minimum, Jugal Kishor ji.'

Jugal replied with finality in his tone, '4000 men, 200 horses, twenty cannons and 100 camels.'

'But it is not even half of what I demanded!' said Sardar angrily.

'You asked for an army that would drain our reserves, Sardar Khan. With an army of the size you demanded, are you going to attack two small kingdoms or are you planning to wage a war against Ahmad Shah Abdali himself?' Jugal remained calm and kept smiling, which infuriated Sardar even further.

'Let me remind you that the size of the Vijaygarh and Haripur armies combined is much larger than what I need,' retaliated Sardar.

'How are you so sure the armies will combine forces?' asked Jugal, questioning Sardar Khan's intelligence.

Sardar's dark eyes narrowed. 'We cannot leave anything to chance. We need brutality and strength in numbers.'

'But the same result can be achieved with half those numbers,' Jugal's voice was still calm.

'I disagree!' Sardar retorted. 'I say we overwhelm them with numbers . . . break their spirits merely by the size of our force.'

'Overwhelming them is one way, but there are other ways,' Jugal replied cryptically.

'Your secretive ways, it's frustrating!' Sardar shouted, his patience thinning. 'We need action, not confusion.'

Jugal Kishore looked away as though Sardar was invisible, then signalled a guard, who was armed with a javelin and standing at the entrance of the tent, to come and stand in front of Sardar Khan.

'With the size of the army you demand, even this guard can win Vijaygarh and Haripur for us,' said Jugal, pointing at the soldier. 'What is the need when the great commander Sardar Khan is leading?' continued Jugal, taunting Sardar Khan. 'Tactics, Sardar, not confusion. It's not always about strength.'

'Tactics! Your tactics are like a riddle wrapped in a mystery! This is war!' Sardar growled, his face red with rage from Jugal's consistent humiliation.

'War is the grandest riddle, Sardar. Solve it right and victory is yours,' Jugal retorted coolly, not breaking eye contact.

'Have it your way, but remember, if we lose this battle, it will be on your hands,' Sardar warned, turning on his heel to leave.

'You're wrong about that. It seems to be a win–win for me. Either you return victorious, proving me right about the size of the army granted to you, or you never return, proving me victorious yet again.'

Sardar's eyes filled with outrage, and Jugal Kishore smiled and said, 'It was a joke, just to make the tent lighter of your weight.' Pointing towards himself, Jugal continued, 'May the right be victorious.' He then started to laugh loudly, indicating that Sardar leave.

Sardar Khan knew this was yet another cryptic remark, disguised as a joke and garnished with a smile. His frustration was visible in his eyes as he left the tent. The flaps fell back with a loud snap.

Alone again, Jugal allowed a slight smirk to grace his face. He turned to his assistant, instructing him to begin a letter.

Meanwhile, outside the tent, the grim reality of the raid unveiled itself. Sardar Khan strode through the aftermath of the attack, passing Abdali's troops who revelled in the despair of their captives. Hindu men, bound and helpless, were subjected to unspeakable torment, their agonized screams tearing through the heavy air. Women were being herded towards other tents, their faces pale and stricken with terror. The horrifying scene was a stark contrast to the calculated conversation that had taken place within the confines of the grand camp.

Meanwhile, the sky over Vijaygarh was ablaze with thousands of twinkling diyas, their warm glow reflecting the grandeur and beauty of their tradition and culture.

Standing in the grand hall of his towering fortress, King Manohar of Vijaygarh took in the view. His hair had started losing colour to snowy white strands and his wrinkles had deepened around his eyes and lips. He had a sturdy build, hinting at years spent at war, and a calm and patient demeanour that he had developed while dedicating his life to his kingdom. He was known for being a wise leader and a benevolent ruler with a deep respect for tradition.

Just then, the young king of Haripur, Vedant, who was wealthy and ambitious, arrived. Unlike Manohar, Vedant's skin had a youthful radiance and his eyes were full of life and sparkle. He had a lean frame and looked like a hawk. His sharp features and jet-black hair contrasted starkly with his brilliant white attire. Vedant had taken charge of the kingdom very young due to his father's untimely demise, and he was known for his ambitious ruling style. The old king and the young sat facing each other, worry evident on Manohar's face.

'Thank you for inviting me to your beautiful kingdom, King Manohar,' Vedant greeted him, his eyes taking in the festivities below.

'The beauty is not in the kingdom but in the people living in it,' said King Manohar.

'They find joy even in the darkest times. This kingdom is their accomplishment,' he continued, a tinge of worry edging his voice. A pause lingered between the two kings. Both men understood the unstated concern they shared.

'There is no certainty in war,' Vedant finally broke the silence, his eyes meeting Manohar's. 'Every king must make sacrifices.'

Manohar nodded, the echo of personal losses he'd borne for his kingdom over the years ringing in his mind. 'Every king must also carry the burden of those sacrifices.'

'And yet, doubt remains. Will these sacrifices ensure victory?' Vedant inquired.

'No. But it ensures we fought with honour,' Manohar replied.

During their conversation, a private messenger with fearful eyes and trembling lips rushed towards them.

'Maharaj,' he stammered, 'we have information on Sardar Khan's forces. They march towards us. They will be upon us in three days.'

The calm atmosphere outside the room seemed a world away as the young Vedant stood up and extended his hand towards King Manohar.

'Each and every person of your kingdom survived on half a belly of food for my people during Haripur's drought. We owe that to you, King Manohar,' said Vedant. King Manohar proudly and confidently reciprocated, 'There are countless such instances when your father and I stood by each other in times of need. Because of this, Vijaygarh and Haripur have a unique history of never being defeated in any war. Once again, in these trying times, let our kingdoms stand together. Someone must take a stand to stop Abdali in his pursuit, or he will have every last Hindu kingdom wiped out in the blink of an eye. I am certain that together, we will be able to defeat his forces led by Sardar Khan.'

'I know my father would've fought alongside Vijaygarh,' said Vedant, taking Manohar's hand, his gaze meeting Manohar's.

'Your words give me strength. Vijaygarh will not forget this act of solidarity,' said Manohar, feeling some relief.

'Now please allow me to go back to Haripur in order to return before it is time to welcome our common enemy,' requested Vedant.

As Vedant took his leave, Manohar turned to his advisors, his voice a low thunder, 'The Afghans are coming to Vijaygarh in three days. Prepare the troops for war. Vijaygarh and Haripur will once again fight together.' Despite the cheer and celebrations that filled the air of Vijaygarh, within the fortress walls, a war was being planned, alliances being forged and lives being put at stake.

Haripur's commander in chief, Krishna looked at his young king Vedant confidently and said, 'According to the information received, Sardar Khan's marching army to Vijaygarh is 4000 men, 200 horses, twenty cannons and 100 camels, my king. On our side, we have 2700 soldiers, 100 elephants, 150 horses and ten moveable cannons. Vijaygarh's army is around 3000 men, 50 elephants, 50 horses and ten cannons.' Vedant looked at his commander in chief, Krishna, whose eyes were filled with confidence.

'My king, the warriors of Haripur and Vijaygarh together are ready. If we fight alongside Vijaygarh, our victory is inevitable. Please allow us to bring Sardar Khan to his knees and gift his head to you. Rest assured that this will stand as a warning to the invaders to never step foot in our land again.'

In reply, Vedant calmly stood from his thrown and addressed his assembly: 'Haripur will not participate in the war alongside Vijaygarh.'

'But why, my king?' asked Krishna, his confidence crushed. Vedant extended his hand and passed a scroll to Krishna.

The letter laid out a tempting offer. 'King Vedant, I extend a hand of gratitude and friendship towards Haripur. King Manohar's defeat is certain. It's your decision now whether to help a dead king with all your men on the line or to shake hands with the Afghan army. In return, I promise that the Afghans will never lay a hand on your kingdom. Please consider this letter our written assurance of this pact. I will await your answer.'

'My king, this could be a trap. We cannot trust these Afghans. Your father would never do this as the king,' said Krishna to Vedant.

'As a king, the lives of my people come first. I will do whatever it takes to safeguard my people and save my kingdom. My father is dead and has left me, his son, in charge. Who faces the burden of protecting every single man of the kingdom? Who faces the burden of defeat? Surely not a dead man.'

Shocked, Krishna tried to reason with Vedant: 'But, my king . . .'

'This is not a discussion, this is a decision that has already been made, Krishna!' exclaimed Vedant in a commanding tone. The disappointment and guilt of not helping King Manohar was clear on Krishna's face.

Vedant then quickly demanded parchment and quill. Dipping his quill in black ink, he wrote: 'I am deeply honoured by the offer of an alliance from a leader of your strength, stature and intelligence. I accept your offer and assure you that this union will benefit you enormously. You will be satisfied by Haripur. Vijaygarh will be all yours.'

Krishna's face was filled with disappointment, guilt, helplessness and the pain of disloyalty towards an allied kingdom.

Back in Vijaygarh, three days passed in tense anticipation. The setting sun decorated the skyline with hues of fire as King Manohar stood at the forefront of his army, a striking image of courage and resilience. The ground beneath them vibrated with the combined might of their cavalry, a mix of prancing horses and majestic elephants outfitted for battle. Men of varying ages, their faces hardened by determination, grasped their weapons, be it swords, arrows or daggers, with a grip of unwavering resolve.

Despite the prospect of war, the sight of his people ready to defend their homeland instilled a sense of pride in Manohar. His heart fluttered in his chest like a caged bird, but his expression bore the calm of a seasoned leader. His eyes, usually warm and inviting, now had the chilling look of a soldier, ready for the battle ahead.

'How long will Haripur's army take to reach and join our forces?' King Manohar asked his army commander.

With his head hanging low, the commander replied, 'My Lord, they are not coming.'

Manohar's calm was shattered by the news of Vedant's treachery. Haripur, his trusted ally, had turned its back on him. Saddened by this betrayal, Manohar wanted to find peace for his people now. What was meant to be a promising win was suddenly a suicide mission for every man standing there, trusting his king.

Concealing his shock and disappointment, he turned to his messenger, his voice steady yet ringing with a sense of urgency. 'Fetch me parchment and ink,' he commanded. He chose ink over blood and words over war. His fingers, hardened from years of sword fighting, grasped the quill as he himself began to pen a message to Sardar Khan, each word bearing the weight of his kingdom's fate. This message was his last effort to save his people, and despite the turmoil within him, his determination remained unbroken. He knew he could afford neither fear nor despair in this test of fire and blood—only the hope of peace for his men, women and children.

The messengers, entrusted with this offer of a truce, found their way to Sardar Khan's camp.

Ajaa and Shambhu ji, though on separate paths, were now only a day's journey away from Gokul. Ajaa's wait shortened with each step—it had been months since he had last seen Shambhu ji. It was the day before Shukla paksha and the streets of Gokul had already started brimming with Naga sadhus and sadhvis. Camps had been set up all over the town to provide food and shelter. The residents of Gokul also participated with zeal in the preparations for the grand puja the next day and welcomed the Naga sadhus with respect and gratitude.

Meanwhile, not far from the fort of Vijaygarh, Sardar's army was preparing to attack. Two messengers hurried into Sardar's tent, carrying King Manohar's message. After receiving the letter, Sardar Khan agreed to discuss his terms for peace with Manohar and an invitation welcoming Manohar into Sardar Khan's tent was sent back to Manohar through his own messengers.

King Manohar arrived at Sardar's base tent, as requested in the letter. The blustering wind caused the heavy tent to rustle loudly. Along with Manohar, a small band of soldiers had arrived to indicate his faith and confidence that an agreement of truce could indeed be settled between the two. King Manohar and Sardar Khan sat facing each other. A volatile tension sparked between them.

Breaking the silence in the camp, King Manohar greeted Sardar: 'I am grateful for your reply, Sardar Khan, and that we now sit facing each other.' Sardar smiled as if wanting to hear more. 'I might lose the battle, but this will lead to thousands of your men getting killed too. Sardar Khan, let's be responsible and wise towards our men, who trust us with their lives.'

'Men will die, and men will come. I do not bother, this is war,' answered Sardar, making sure that Manohar understood his intentions.

King Manohar stood up, went closer to Sardar Khan and offered him his sword. 'The people of my kingdom are my family. This sword is my honour. Now tell me what you want in exchange for the lives of all my men and children.'

Sardar calmly accepted King Manohar's sword and then signalled to his soldiers to grab the king by his arms. The unarmed king was forced to his knees by repeated punches to his back and then made to bow, lowering his head until his forehead touched the ground. Sardar pulled out Manohar's own sword, knelt beside the king and said, '*Bismillah, Allahu Akbar* (in the name of Allah, Allah is the greatest).'

And then, he held Manohar's hair in one hand and cut his throat with his own sword. King Manohar struggled to free himself but Sardar Khan cut open his windpipe and all the veins in his neck until Manohar's head was completely separated from his body. Sardar Khan lifted his head, still holding it from the hair, brought it closer to his own face and said, 'Why did you even think that I would settle for anything less than everything?' He then ordered his soldiers to kill the rest of Manohar's men waiting outside.

'Commence attack on Vijaygarh. The fort must fall by noon,' Sardar Khan ordered his commanders and walked out of the tent with King Manohar's head.

5

Vanraaj

While Ajaa started his journey to Gokul from the waterfall and Shambhu ji from Maheshwar, in a small village near Gokul, a man stood tall, surrounded by an anxious bunch of villagers. He stood outside a tiny, weather-beaten hut. The man seemed to be in his late forties. He had a round face, rosy cheeks, dewy eyes, a button nose and a mischievous smile. His eyes were fixed on a venomous, hissing snake, coiled on the hut's thatched roof. Everyone around him seemed afraid, but the man was calm. A playful grin highlighted his chubby features as he gently approached the snake, extending his hand.

'All right, all right, Vasuki Dev,' he charmed the snake in a friendly voice. 'Time to get off the roof, wouldn't you say?' His conduct contrasted starkly with the tense situation, his jovial tone oddly comforting.

The man was a sight to behold, with his solid and sturdy arms. Yet, a round potbelly added an amusing characteristic to his personality. As the snake finally slithered down, the crowd gasped in fear. Children covered their eyes with their palms and the women bit their lips. However, the man remained composed and extended his arm, inviting the serpent to coil around it, which it did, up from his right hand, across his neck and down to his left arm. People looking at this spectacle let their hearts skip a beat wondering what if the snake attacked the man while it was coiled around his neck and face?

He was carrying a heavy bag in his left hand which he calmly opened and the snake got into it. Silence hung over the villagers, and then it broke as they burst into applause. The man took a bow and waved his hands in the air like an achiever and his laughter mingled with the villagers.

As he walked to the village outskirts with the bag in one hand, the crowd followed. Waiting for him was a towering female elephant and her adorable tiny calf. The female elephant had bags hanging from her back on each side. Just when the man was about to reach the female elephant, Golu, the calf, started jumping up on him in excitement. Trumpeting, Golu shook his head and flapped his ears while continuously trying to jump up on him. The man hugged and petted Golu.

A small boy rushed up, curiosity gleaming in his eyes. 'Where are you taking the snake?' he asked.

'I am taking him home, little one,' the man replied, a soft smile playing on his lips. 'Back to the forest . . . to its rightful place.'

Climbing on to the female elephant, he patted her head and said, 'Now, you know where to go, Dulari; shall we?' As Dulari trundled on, a pretty neelkanth (Indian roller) fluttered down, perching on the man's shoulder. The beautiful bird, named after one of the many names of Shiva—from the Sanskrit words '*neel*', meaning blue, and '*kanth*', meaning throat—flaunted an alluring array of colours. Its crown was a rich shade of turquoise blue and its wings showcased a mesmerizing mix of deep purples, bright blues and aquamarines. Its bright blue throat stood out against a brownish body, allowing the vibrant blue to pop. Its stout, slightly curved beak was a muted yellow and the bird's eyes were penetrating, dark, alert and always scanning its surroundings. The snake catcher raised a hand, gently stroking its soft feathers.

The view was breathtaking as the golden light of the setting sun spread across the sky. The man sitting on the towering female elephant, a serpent in a bag, a bird on his shoulder and Golu the elephant calf marched towards the horizon. His affection towards the animals made it impossible not to be drawn towards his compassionate spirit and pleasant nature. The harmony between him and the creatures around him painted a vivid picture of the colourful world he lived in, leaving all the villagers mesmerized and in awe of his unique charm. The kids following him out of the village screamed and asked, 'Baba! Who are you?'

'I am a friend of the forest; Vanraaj is what everybody calls me!' he answered without looking back and waved as the kids ran after him, cheering and clapping.

The sun was about to set. Vanraaj patted Dulari's head and said, 'Why don't you teach your cute little Golu some

etiquette? Look what he has done to my dress! She has spoilt
it.' They marched ahead.

Thirsty Vanraaj, Dulari and her son Golu had been on
the move for a few hours. Tired from the dust and the
heat, they halted by a stream. Leaving the elephants to graze
nearby, he bent to fill his flask. A distant rhythmic pounding
drew his attention. His eyes darted across the foliage,
catching sight of a tide of bodies moving in unity—a wave
of Naga sadhus, their ash-smeared forms seeming spectral in
the shimmering heat.

This sight aroused Vanraaj's curiosity. It wasn't the
season for the Kumbh Mela or any other significant religious
event. Yet, a group of Naga sadhus was on the move.
Intrigued, Vanraaj subtly shadowed them, with Dulari and
Golu following quietly.

He caught snippets of their conversation from his cover
behind a thick tree. 'Shukla paksha . . . important meeting . . .
Gokul . . . ,' they murmured among themselves. The name
'Gokul' sparked excitement in Vanraaj's eyes—he knew he
had to dig deeper.

A rustle of leaves under Dulari's feet betrayed his
presence as he contemplated his next move. A Naga sadhu
named Narayan found him hiding behind the tree. Although
he seemed about the same age as Vanraaj, his more than 7
feet tall toned body, tangled dreadlocks and coarse features,
indicating years of strictness and discipline, were a sharp
contrast to Vanraaj's friendly features. Vanraaj rose to his
feet, his face reflecting sincerity and respect.

'Who are you and what are you doing here?' asked Narayan angrily.

'Namaste, sadhu baba. I am just a harmless wanderer. Forests are my home,' Vanraaj replied, with his hands joined in respect.

Narayan said, with his one eyebrow raised, 'Even so, it is not polite to eavesdrop on other people's conversations.'

'I'm so sorry, sadhu baba, I didn't mean to intrude or disturb, but I have always been fascinated by Naga sadhus and their gatherings. Is there a mela in Gokul? And if so, could I join you on your journey?' Vanraaj requested eagerly.

The Naga sadhu's gaze was steely, evaluating Vanraaj for a moment before he gestured dismissively. 'You are not one of us. This is not a path for you. Leave,' he instructed in his gravelly voice.

Vanraaj looked at the Naga and tried one last time to convince him. He said politely, 'I will be useful. I just wish to serve you all and get your blessings. Please take me with you. I will massage your feet as well.' Narayan shook his head in refusal.

Disheartened, Vanraaj bowed his head in acceptance, but with disappointment. He was a man of free will and even though he barely interacted with any humans, his rejection by the Nagas was hurtful. The Naga sadhus continued their journey towards Gokul, leaving Vanraaj in the jungle.

As the day faded, Narayan's words kept echoing in Vanraaj's mind 'You are not one of us', igniting within him a desire to prove himself. Vanraaj's mind was already charting a course. Whatever this mystery was, he wanted to uncover it.

However, after a few hours, Vanraaj's childish soul could no longer contain his curiosity.

'Dulari, what harm could it do to go and have a look?' he said to the elephant and then turned her towards Gokul and said, patting her head, 'Dulari, now you know where to go.'

Dulari started walking towards Gokul. Perched on Dulari, followed by Golu, Vanraaj followed Narayan and the other Nagas on the path to Gokul.

6

Gokul

'Was Gokul a special place, then?' asked the hiker, Thomas.

'Gokul is still a special place and will remain so till the end of the world,' replied the nameless Naga with a smile on his face.

'What's so special about this place Gokul?'

The nameless Naga continued: A place that earned its salvation by Lord Krishna's hands himself will always be special. In the ancient town of Gokul, there lived a cruel king named Kansa. His rule was marked by fear and suffering as he imposed heavy taxes and subjected the people to his ruthless whims. Yet, little did Kansa know that his reign of terror was destined to meet its end.

A prophecy had foretold the birth of a child who would be his demise. That child was none other than Lord Krishna, the divine avatar of Vishnu. Krishna's parents, Devaki and Vasudeva, were locked away in a prison cell by Kansa, as it was prophesied that their eighth child would bring about his downfall. Each time Devaki gave birth, Kans mercilessly took the child and ended its life.

However, when Krishna was born, a divine intervention occurred. Miraculously, the prison doors opened, and Vasudeva was able to carry the newborn Krishna to safety across the raging Yamuna River to the village of Gokul. There, he exchanged Krishna with a baby girl, Yashoda's newborn, and returned to the prison without arousing suspicion.

Later, when Kans came to kill the baby girl, she flew from his hand, revealed herself as Maya and vanished after telling Kansa that his death was inevitable.

Krishna grew up in Gokul as a cowherd, endearing himself to everyone with his charm, mischief and divine exploits. As he matured, his extraordinary powers became evident and his reputation as the embodiment of grace and righteousness spread far and wide.

When Kansa learnt of Krishna's existence and the prophecy, he unleashed a series of demons and wicked schemes to eliminate the divine child. Krishna fearlessly faced each challenge, defeating demons like Putana, Trinavarta and Keshi.

Finally, the day of reckoning arrived. Krishna, having come of age, confronted Kansa in a mighty showdown. With his divine strength and cunning, Krishna overpowered Kansa and cast him from his throne. The prophecy had come true, and Gokul was freed from Kansa's oppressive rule.

Krishna's birth and his victory over Kansa became a symbol of hope and divine intervention for all, a reminder that righteousness and courage would always triumph over tyranny. Krishna's legacy endured, and his teachings on love, morality and devotion continue to inspire countless souls to this day.

Even in the 1750s, this divine connection was evident in every aspect of Gokul.

Houses made of mud and straw lined the narrow, unpaved streets, their walls often adorned with colourful murals depicting scenes from Krishna's childhood. As one walked the complicated pathways, the aroma of incense and freshly cooked meals wafted out from windows, creating a heady mix of scents.

The centre of Gokul was dominated by majestic havelis and temples, each more intricate and richly decorated than the last. The temples were characterized by their towering shikharas and bore the fine craftsmanship of the region, with intricate carvings and delicate work. The continuous tolling of temple bells added to the rhythmic chanting of prayers, and the soulful melodies of devotional songs were a constant backdrop to the hustle and bustle of everyday life.

Thanks to the nourishing Yamuna, the town was wrapped in an emerald quilt of fertile farmland. Many residents were engaged in farming and animal husbandry, with herds of cattle being a common sight. The daily life of Gokul in the 1750s was naturally tied to the rhythm of nature.

Despite being a small town, Gokul was a melting pot of cultures. The music of birds chirping and cows mooing and the vibrant colours of the textiles created a lively atmosphere, as if Krishna still lived there.

The region's local traditions were harmoniously interwoven with influences from across the country, brought in by the many pilgrims and travellers who visited this holy town. Festivals, especially those related to Lord Krishna, were grand affairs celebrated enthusiastically, transforming the village into a spectacle of lights, colours and joyous revelry.

Life in Gokul in the 1750s was humble and simple, yet imbued with a profound sense of spirituality and community. Amid the rhythm of daily chores and routines, a sense of calm and peace prevailed, underpinned by the town's unshakeable faith in the divine.

The atmosphere in Gokul shifted palpably as the sun's glow turned a deeper shade of amber. A gentle hum of activity started to reverberate through its streets and meadows. From the outskirts, a stream of figures could be seen approaching. At first, they were distant silhouettes against the waning daylight, but as they came closer, their identities became clear.

Naga sadhus, their lean bodies smeared with ash and adorned with rudraksh beads, began to fill the grounds. Their dreadlocks, matted from years of ascetic practice, trailed behind them or were coiled atop their heads. Every step they took was a testament to years of dedication, sacrifice and unwavering faith. Close on their heels, sadhvis dressed in vibrant saffron, their foreheads marked with sacred tilaks, flowed into the village like a river of devotion. They moved with a grace and purpose that spoke of their spiritual journey. Although not subjected to the same rigorous training as the Naga sadhus, their commitment to dharma and the divine was just as profound.

Ajaa stepped on to the soft grass of Gokul, his bare feet relishing the cool touch after his arduous journey. The horizon was covered with the golden hues of the setting sun, making long shadows of trees and dwellings alike. In this tranquil setting, a familiar figure caught Ajaa's eye. Sitting in contemplation under an ancient banyan tree was none other than his revered guru, Shambhu ji. 'Shambhu ji!' Ajaa exclaimed, smiling, looking at Shambhu ji as a son looks at his father after returning from a long journey abroad.

Shambhu ji's face broke into a broad smile upon seeing his favourite protege, his wrinkles deepening like the grooves of an old tree. 'Ajaa!' he exhaled with relief, rising to his feet, while Ajaa bent to touch his feet for blessings. They hugged each other, their bond palpable.

As the initial joy waned, a weighty silence settled between them. Gokul's serenity contrasted sharply with the tension evident on Ajaa and Shambhu ji's faces.

'You've heard?' Shambhu ji's voice was low, almost a whisper, as if uttering it louder would make the looming reality even more tangible.

Ajaa nodded, his determined eyes unwavering. 'The whispers of Afghani troops and their unspeakable brutalities have travelled far. The screams of the painful deaths in the dark smoke of winds carry their stories.'

Shambhu ji looked deeply into his pupil's eyes, a hint of worry clouding his own. 'War is coming, it seems.' Ajaa's face remained calm, but a fire burned in his eyes.

They both sat in silence. No more words needed to be spoken between them any more.

Shambhu ji could see in Ajaa's eyes that he had been preparing. Ajaa could see in Shambhu ji's gaze that every chant, every meditation, every rigorous training session he was put through by Shambhu ji had been undertaken with this destiny in mind.

They sat in peace with the profound realization that stopping this storm was Ajaa's purpose in life, and preparing Ajaa was Shambu ji's.

Ajaa placed a reassuring hand on his guru's shoulder, as if comforting him with his unsaid words: 'Your teachings have been my anchor, Shambhu ji. I'm ready.'

The older sadhu gazed affectionately at his disciple, as if answering with his silence: 'You are my spirit.'

The two sat there, the weight of the upcoming war pressing down upon them. Yet, despite the tension, there was a palpable sense of hope that comes from unwavering determination and faith in one's destiny. The world of Gokul was about to change, but the spirit of its defenders, like Ajaa, remained resolute.

The temples in Gokul in the 1700s were more than mere places of worship. They were centres of learning and culture where the ancient scriptures were taught and studied. The most prominent temples of Gokul were the Gokulnath temple, the Raja Thakur temple and the Madan Mohan temple. Music, dance and drama performances often took place within the temple precincts, making them the cultural hubs of the town.

Despite the ravages of time and various invasions, these temples remained standing, a testament to the period's religious advancement and architectural prowess. That night, every stone, every carving seemed to echo tales from a bygone era, infusing the atmosphere with a profound sense of devotion and reverence. The night was of Shukla paksha.

Thomas's face was scrunched up in thought. 'Shukla paksha? What does that mean?'

Shukla paksha! It's a term from our Hindu tradition. The lunar month is divided into two halves in Hinduism. When the moon grows brighter each night in the first fortnight, it is known as Shukla paksha or the bright half. In the second fortnight, when the moon is waning, it is known as Krishna paksha or the dark half.

And why is the first day of Shukla paksha so important?

The first day of Shukla paksha, when you can barely see a tiny sliver of the moon, is known as Pratipada. On that day, we observe Chandra Darshan. We pray to Chandra Dev, the moon god, seeking his blessings.

It's believed that Chandra Dev brings us prosperity, success and peace of mind. Observing Chandra Darshan is a way for us to connect with the divine and express gratitude for the abundance in our lives. Plus, in astrology, the moon is associated with our emotions, so it helps keep our feelings balanced.

It takes the moon twenty-nine days to complete one revolution around the earth, and the moon's gravity is so strong that it causes the seas on earth to rise and fall. These tides affect our ecosystem and play a significant role in the weather conditions during different seasons. These affect the life cycle of many marine species and even animals on land. One must sit and meditate on the night of Krishna paksha as the moon's pull is strongest that night. Sitting in meditation and keeping the spine erect will cause significant spiritual growth and the person doing so could even attain enlightenment.

The sadhus and sadhvis gather for special rituals and prayers. They chant mantras and seek blessings from the gods. It's a powerful time, especially under the blessings of Lord Shiva, to whom many of these sadhus dedicate their lives.

'But why Lord Shiva?' asked the hiker.

The nameless Naga continued: Shukla paksha is closely associated with Lord Shiva, the cosmic dancer and the destroyer of evil. Pratipada holds a special significance in our Hindu tradition. It is believed that on this day, Lord Shiva and Goddess Parvati began their divine dance of creation, destruction and regeneration. Lord Shiva is considered to be the lord of time and change. The moon's cycle and its phases symbolize the cycles of life, death and rebirth governed by Lord Shiva.

The crescent moon had ascended higher, its soft glow lending a silver sheen to the flowing river. The energy of these nights, combined with the blessings of Shiva, can bring about great transformation and renewal. Many devotees fast and perform puja to seek his blessings.

'So basically, it's a tradition of fasting and prayers,' said the hiker, simplifying it in his head.

'It's not just about praying and fasting, Thomas. It's about appreciating the beauty and magic of the universe around us. Remember, each phase of the moon has its charm and significance, just like every stage of our life.'

As he concluded, the night seemed to come alive with his words. Thomas's gaze fell once again on the bright white mountains, now bathed in soft silvery light. He felt a new-found respect for the moon, Lord Shiva and the profound wisdom embedded in this culture.

Back in Gokul that night, feeling the pull of his duties, Ajaa turned to Shambhu ji with a respectful look in his eyes. 'Shambhu ji, with your permission, I wish to retreat for meditation and prepare for tonight's rituals.'

Shambhu ji nodded, the pride evident in his gaze. 'Go, son. Harness the energy of Shukla paksha and let Lord Shiva guide your spirit.'

With a bow, Ajaa retreated, leaving behind the growing hum of activity in Gokul, readying himself for the sacred night ahead.

In the heart of Gokul, a sacred ceremony was underway. A large pit had been dug in the ground and many people had gathered around it, their faces lit by the warm, dancing flames of the havan or sacred fire. The Mathadhish, the leader of the Naga sadhus, took centre stage. Around him the Naga sadhus sat cross-legged, their focus on the havan.

The Mathadhish's eyes scanned the crowd, pausing to acknowledge the determined and the doubtful. His voice took on a deeper, more urgent tone, 'Today, more than ever, we need to remember the purpose of our creation, roots and existence. We are not mere ascetics. We are the protectors of dharma, the army of Shiva under the banner of Shankaracharya, who have known forever that this night will come.

'In these trying times, we need a man with wisdom and valour, courage and confidence, faith and foresight. Therefore, I have decided to choose Ajaa as our commander. Lend him your trust, your unwavering faith, for the challenge we face is monumental.'

Ajaa stepped into the centre, the weight of the mantle of leadership settling on his shoulders.

Suddenly, the hooves of a horse were heard approaching the Naga men in Gokul. All the Nagas turned towards the sound. A man pale as death, splattered with dried blood, was clinging desperately to the horse's reins.

Shambhu ji's keen eyes scanned the approaching figure and a flash of recognition crossed his face. He quickly stood, shouting commands to clear the path. 'Make way!' he yelled.

As the horse cantered into the clearing, its strides grew slower, perhaps sensing the journey's end. The rider's strength waned with each step, his grip loosened when the horse finally halted and the world tilted. He felt the hold of solid arms just before the darkness of death threatened to claim him.

'Dhruv!' Shambhu ji's voice was filled with shock and concern.

As the edges of his vision dimmed, he gathered his last ounce of energy to convey the dire message that had driven him to Gokul. His voice, weak and husky, barely reached Shambhu ji's ears. He could feel Shambhu ji's grip tighten around him, sensing the gravity of his words.

'They . . . they are coming to Gokul,' Dhruv struggled to articulate, each word draining his remaining strength. 'They will not spare anyone . . . they will . . . kill every last one of you. Two nights . . . only two nights . . . they are coming . . .'

'Who?' asked Ajaa, stepping forward.

Dhruv, still looking at Shambhu ji, replied, 'The Afghan army.'

The weight of Dhruv's revelation seemed to hang in the air as his consciousness slipped away, leaving him in the dark abyss of exhaustion.

There was an uncomfortable shift in the crowd, and a thick tension blanketed the gathering. Murmurs and nervous whispers spread like wildfire, with the villagers and Nagas trying to piece together what had just transpired.

Shambhu ji, with a tight grip on Dhruv's unconscious body, turned to Ajaa, his face filled with concern and determination.

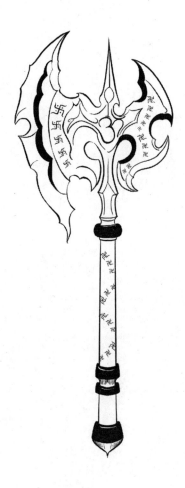

7

Revenge and Realization

Dhruv lay inside a dimly lit hut in Gokul. The sadhvis had dedicated themselves to his recovery, and he could feel some of his strength return. Dhruv shifted slightly. He could feel where the sadhvis had meticulously stitched his torn flesh back together. Their gentle hands, guided by years of learning, had used a combination of sacred herbs and traditional healing techniques. The remedies were already showing their miraculous effects and the pain had subsided slightly. Dhruv could feel a cooling sensation where the medicinal pastes had been applied. Dried blood, a crusty testament to his escape, clung stubbornly to his chest, arms and forehead.

As Dhruv lay there, Ajaa and Shambhu ji arrived at his side. Ajaa's strong presence was unmissable, his silhouette framed against the doorway, his eyes full of concern. His face was smeared with holy ash from the morning prayers. Yet even the ash couldn't mask the softness in his eyes, a hint of the deep empathy and compassion that lay within. His dreadlocks, signifying his detachment from all that was worldly, hung heavily, depicting the weight of the impending battle on his heart.

'Dhruv, tell me everything,' Shambhu ji said, his voice barely above a whisper.

Dhruv took a deep breath as the memories flooded in.

'A day after you left,' said Dhruv, looking at Shambhu ji, 'one of Abdali's smaller units was passing Maheshwar. I was engrossed with my teaching and my students were attentively following the lessons when the tranquil atmosphere of the gurukul was interrupted by a sudden, deafening commotion from the village.

'My heart pounding, I ran towards the village to investigate. A horrifying scene unfolded in front of my eyes. Afghan soldiers were in a killing frenzy, their swords gleaming in the harsh sunlight, as they relentlessly slaughtered the helpless villagers.

'A dark figure in the thick of the turmoil commanded attention. The young Afghan leader stood in the front, dressed in dark leather, a turban on his head and a fur cape marking his rank. Pointing a lethal-looking sword, he raised his arm, directing the soldiers towards the gurukul.

'He was a tower of menace with smouldering amber eyes. His weathered face, with sharp cheekbones and a firm jaw, was hidden behind a wild black beard and messy locks. He was a horrifying blend of ruthless power and looming terror, ready to strike the innocent. Panic gripped my entire being as I began to sprint back towards my students, desperate to shield them from the impending danger.

'Suddenly, a sharp, searing pain shot through my back as a cruel laugh echoed behind me, while a warrior who had been racing after me on a horse headed towards my little, innocent students. I collapsed to the ground and fell unconscious. I could hear the cries of my children even in my unconscious state. I can still hear them calling for mercy and help.' Dhruv took a break, unable to breathe, his heart unbearably heavy. Shambhu ji and Ajaa looked at each other, rage in their eyes.

Dhruv took a deep breath to be able to speak again, 'When I opened my eyes, I found myself lying on a mat, my back wrapped in clean bandages. The sting of healing herbs prickled my wounds. A *vaidya* was sitting by my side, stirring a pot of medicinal brew.

'Gathering my strength, I asked him about the villagers and my students. The vaidya merely looked at me with sorrowful eyes and remained silent. My heart sank and I knew I needed to see things for myself.

'Supporting myself against the walls of the hut, I somehow managed to get to my feet. Each step towards the gurukul an agonizing trial of physical and emotional endurance. When I arrived, my heart was shattered into a thousand pieces. The courtyard was eerily silent. The bodies of my beloved students lay strewn all over, their lives extinguished prematurely. The female students were nowhere to be seen.

'I fell to my knees and started wailing and crying helplessly, my screams echoing through the silent village.

My tears mingled with the soil of the gurukul as I mourned the senseless loss. I have failed my people. "What meaning or purpose is there to my existence?" I thought as I lay there, crying and motionless.

'I would have ended my life that night but despite the grief, a spark ignited within me as I remembered your words, Shambhu ji.

'Before leaving my gurukul, you had said, "The invaders won't disappear by erasing just the word on a board. You too need to lift your weapon to erase them in real life. Never forget that even our gods needed weapons when they were attacked by the asuras. We all are children of the gods, how can we think that we won't need weapons? Think about it when you have time."

'With a new-found purpose, I pushed myself up, my eyes blazing in a fiery wrath for my new mission. The time for peace had passed; now was the time for retaliation. I picked up an axe and set off to find and kill those men and their commander. It was easy to track those asuras. I just followed the trail of death and destruction, because that was all they left behind.'

Shambhu ji had a curious look on his face . 'How did you get hold of a horse? Maheshwar to Gokul is a long journey.'

Dhruv replied, 'To avenge my students' death, I was in search of the enemy troops when I came upon Sardar Khan's men ruining Vijaygarh. They had reduced it to smouldering waste within hours. Fire devoured the once majestic fortress, flames dancing mercilessly over the bodies of the brave troops, who lay lifeless. The air had turned thick with smoke and despair. I followed the Afghans at a distance to Sardar's camp. His camp was as large as an entire city, lined with black tents of all sizes and soldiers and animals as far as the eye could see. It was a dark abyss in a land of purity, prosperity and colour, like a cluster of cancer cells slowly swallowing the body's organs, feasting upon their host until it was dead.

'At some distance from me, celebrations were in full swing. Beside a massive fire, a tall pole was staked into the ground, with King Manohar's head fixed atop it. His headless body lay cast aside, unattended, stripped of all its dignity, along with his clothes.

'Shock waves ran through my body at this horrific sight. Seeing a few soldiers passing nearby, I quickly hid behind a tent. There I overheard Sardar Khan and his commanders.

'"I am not satisfied, and I will not rest until I have conquered Haripur as well," Sardar Khan said.

'"*Huzoor*, our troops are thirstier for blood with each victory. If you command it, they will stop at nothing," a commander replied in a meek voice. Sardar Khan seemed pleased with this. "Huzoor, I have a suggestion," another commander said after getting a signal from Sardar Khan to speak. "While our troops prepare to attack Haripur, there is a small town called Gokul that can be reached and raided within a night's detour. That town is rich in temples that are covered in gold. It will be an easy victory and a huge morale booster for our troops."

'"How much gold can we expect from Gokul?" Sardar Khan asked.

'"Huzoor, the more the temples, the more the devotees, the more the devotees, the more the gold reserves inside the temples: minimum 200 kg of gold and countless precious jewels and stones along with men for day's labour and women for night pleasures."

'Sardar seemed impressed and passed his orders, "Then we shall attack Gokul first. I bestow this responsibility on you. Give me news of victory in three days."

'I had overheard the conversation between you and the Nagas in the gurukul that day, and I knew that many of you were gathering in Gokul at this time, unaware of the Afghan plans of attack. I knew then that I had to leave for Gokul immediately to inform you and the other Naga sadhus of this plan. But just then, I saw the young Afghan commander who had ordered my students killed emerge from his tent. The sight of him, calm and basking in his power, fuelled my simmering rage. As he hurried out of sight, I sneaked into his tent, waiting for an opportune moment.

'I found a dagger lying on a table in his tent. On inspecting it, I found it sharp enough for my intentions. I had never thought of myself as a killer. I was a stern teacher but never harsh. I favoured discipline but never raised my voice. I could never even scold or punish a child when they made a mistake. Before this moment, I could barely consider harming any being. However, these Afghan soldiers did not have the same values. They didn't need a reason to slaughter.

'As I waited for the commander in the solitude of the tent, I remained hidden and prepared my plan. I would wait for him to fall asleep and then act. But things went differently. When the commander finally entered the tent, he was in no mood to rest. Outside, I could hear loud cheers at Sardar Khan's victory over Vijaygarh mingled with the screams and cries of the men and women they brought as slaves with them.

'"Bring me the most beautiful women of Vijaygarh," ordered the commander to one of his soldiers. He was moving around the tent restlessly and I decided I would have to make the first move or I would get caught. I jumped on him and held the dagger against his neck. At that moment, I believed my journey would end there and I would not be able to reach Gokul. But I could not leave this opportunity for revenge. As the commander pulled away from me, my stitches tore open and I started bleeding. I finally managed to kill the commander by stabbing his throat, but I was bleeding profusely.

'The commotion had alerted the other soldiers outside the tent. It was my cue to escape. I rushed out from the back of the tent, where it was completely dark. I could hear some horses in the distance, so I crawled towards them.

'I had lost too much blood and was starting to lose consciousness when, somehow, I felt my inner strength return. All the Naga sadhus were gathering at Gokul, unaware of the impending attack. I had to let you know. I don't remember much from after that, but I somehow found a horse and resumed my journey to Gokul.

'I rode like a madman, pushing myself and my faithful steed to our limits. Every inch of my body ached and every drop of strength was sapped. Finally, the horizon started to shimmer, and the outlines of Gokul became visible. My heart raced, not from fatigue but from urgency. I spurred the horse into a gallop, each hoof beat resonating with my pounding heart, announcing our approach.

'I barely registered the reactions around me. My vision was blurred, but I could see the Naga sadhus turning at the sound of my horse, their expressions morphing from curiosity to alarm. I must have presented quite a sight.'

Dhruv looked in Shambhu ji's eyes, his resolve strengthened, 'I have realized that I want to be on the frontlines, fighting alongside all of you.'

Shambhu ji placed a comforting hand on his shoulder and responded firmly, 'Dhruv, your body needs to heal. Rest now.'

8

Gods of War

It was 3 a.m. Gokul was as serene as it was every night, and the village lay in a quiet slumber. A magical aura enveloped the riverside as the silvery moonlight cast a glow upon the gentle waves of the river. However, today was different. It had been a day since Dhruv's warning, and Gokul was under threat. The Naga sadhus gathered at the riverbank. Locals watched from a safe distance with devotion and curiosity.

The silence was punctuated by the soft tinkling of bells. It was time for Bhasmaarti, a ritualistic ode to Lord Shiva and a reminder of life's impermanence. Leading the ritual, the Mathadhish and Ajaa stepped into the cool water, their skin glistening under the moonlight. Shambhu ji, calm as ever, stood beside them, leading the others. It was a mesmerizing moment for Adhiraj and as he blew his shankh, the Naga sadhus, led by Narayan's heavy voice, started chanting the Mahamrityunjaya mantra in a chorus that echoed across the land, air and water.

ॐ त्र्यम्बकं यजामहे सुगन्धिं पुष्टिवर्धनम्।
उर्वारुकमिव बन्धनान्मृत्योर्मुक्षीय माऽमृतात्।।

Om Tryambakam Yajamahe Sugandhim Pushti-
Vardhanam,
Urvarukamiva Bandhanan Mrityormukshiya Maamritat,

(We worship the three-eyed one [Lord Shiva], who is
fragrant and nourishes all. Just like the ripe cucumber
is released from its attachment to the vine, may we be
liberated from death and bestowed with immortality.)

Thereafter, the Mathadhish gave Ajaa a holy bath while
chanting the Yamuna Stotram, marking Ajaa as the leader.

यमुने च यमुने च यमुने च विचरति यत्र कुत्रापि सानन्दम्।
तत्र तत्र सुखं ब्रूयात् यमुना तव जलम् साक्षाद् अमृतम्॥

Yamune cha yamune cha yamune cha vicharati yatra
kutraapi saanandam|
Tatra tatra sukham brooyaat Yamuna tava jalam saakshaad
amritam||

(Wherever one wanders on the banks of the Yamuna,
wherever one bathes in her waters, one experiences true
bliss. The water of the Yamuna is directly the nectar of
immortality.)

All the Naga sadhus threw ash on Ajaa, surrounding him on all sides as he came out of the water. Shambhu ji drew a tripoorn on Ajaa's forehead while everybody continued chanting and Adhiraj continued blowing his shankh.

'Har har Mahadev!' rang out.

Ajaa stepped forward and welcomed everybody with open arms. 'Today,' he spoke, his voice carrying the weight of wisdom and the depth of death, 'we don't live simply as Naga sadhus, but as beings preparing for a divine death, if needed, for the protection of dharma. That is the purpose of our existence. We smear ashes on ourselves so that we and everyone who ever sees us never forgets that, ultimately, this is what we will be: ashes. Ashes that will be put on someone else's body after we are burned, to inspire that being to protect dharma unless he too turns into ashes after his death and mixes with us in rituals and on the next living body. We are not humans having spiritual experiences; we are spiritual beings experiencing human lives. Unlike normal men, we don't wear clothes and ornaments. We are death to the enemies of dharma and we wear them after transforming them to ashes.'

The sacred ash, symbolic of life's transience, was prepared fresh from cremated remains mixed with drops of cow ghee. For the Naga sadhus, this ash was a shield, a protector and a reminder.

Shambhu ji began the process, taking the ash in his palms. He applied it methodically over his body, each stroke accompanied by a sacred mantra.

ॐ नमः शिवाय।

Om Namah Shivaya (I bow to Shiva).

The Mathadhish, Narayan, Adhiraj and all others followed suit. The locals watched in awe as the men transformed themselves, their bodies gleaming silver with the ash, their souls seemingly merging with the divine.

The air was electric with energy. As the last of the ash was applied and the final mantra tapered away, there was a momentary silence. The silence spoke of unity, purpose and the approaching battle.

The dawn was approaching and the first rays of the sun were about to pierce the sky, when Ajaa spoke again: 'Today, we face our first attack. But remember, with the divine on our side, with our unity and our purpose, no force can deter us. You can't die as long as you protect the one standing beside you because the one beside you will do the same and protect you. You don't die as long as he is alive, and he will be alive as long as you don't die. That is what will make all of you immortal and invincible. This is a celebration that heralds the festival of war . . . so rejoice!'

The sky was still dark and the Naga sadhus danced in a furious rhythm and conducted Bhasmaarti with full passion, unaware that two Afghan spies, Farid and Tariq, were hidden in the bushes, on the other side of the riverbank, watching them. They were close enough to see the Nagas clearly, but not to hear the conversation. Farid, a muscular man with just one hand, smirked, 'Look at them! Playing with ash while we prepare to play with their lives tomorrow. These naked, unarmed nomads are no threat.'

Tariq, a bulkier figure with a bald head, chuckled in agreement. 'If they are lucky, they will be gone tomorrow before we raid the town, and if they are not, they will run with their tails between their legs at simply seeing our weapons. Our hundred Afghan warriors can raze this village to the ground in a matter of hours. This town stands as a beautiful, defenceless woman waiting to be claimed by force.'

'Once we have Gokul,' he said with a wicked grin, 'its treasures will fill our reserves, and these sadhus will be a mere footnote in our grand conquest.'

Tariq nodded, looking once more at the Naga sadhus, chanting their mantras by the riverbank. The spectacle of the Bhasmaarti ritual only deepened the duo's conviction of their imminent win.

The spies retreated into the shadows, eagerly awaiting the dawn that promised them an easy victory. As they stood up and walked away, a set of eyes, capable of frightening even the strongest at heart, was looking at them leaving. They were the eyes of a Naga they didn't know was buried in the mud right beside them, camouflaged in the darkness of the night and the colour of the soil. On the orders of Ajaa, he had his eyes closed but ears open, as long as Tariq and Farid stayed there talking.

As Tariq and Farid stood and walked back to their troops to tell them that Gokul was a cake walk, the silently buried Naga sadhu opened his eyes and saw them leaving. The whites of his eyes gleamed in the dark.

The faint light of dawn had begun to paint the horizon with a soft orange hue when a team of a hundred soldiers started their advance towards the city. But as they entered, Gokul appeared abandoned. The streets, usually buzzing with activity, now echoed with a haunting silence. The slight chill of the pre-dawn air and the slowly illuminating sky painted a surreal picture of the village—untouched and pristine.

Sardar Khan's soldiers, wielding menacing swords, silently rode into the heart of Gokul. Their horses' hooves tapped lightly on the cobblestoned streets, the only sound breaking the silence of the morning.

A fleet of horse carriages stood ready. Bullock carts, with their large wooden wheels and sturdy frames, were lined up alongside, to carry the anticipated loot from the temple.

Each cart and carriage bore the emblem of Ahmad Shah Abdali, a symbol recognized and feared throughout the region. The bullocks, sensing the tension in the air, occasionally snorted and stamped while the horses tethered to the carriages flicked their tails and shifted uneasily.

On reaching the grand Kali temple, the soldiers were amazed. They had expected the temple to be bustling with early morning worshippers, especially after a major festival. But it stood grandiose and silent, its hall inviting and vacant.

A single voice intoned the puja in the temple, the sound of the mantras carrying outside. A few soldiers dismounted and cautiously approached the temple entrance. Inside, the flicker of a few remaining oil lamps illuminated the golden deity and the various precious ornaments waiting to be snatched. 'They're probably sleeping off the night's festivities. The fools don't know what's coming,' whispered an Afghan soldier, glancing around suspiciously.

His companion, grinning greedily at the sight of the temple's treasures, responded, 'Let's gather all this gold first. The villagers can wait to die.'

As the soldiers reached the temple door, they started to put down their gear. The sound of swords hitting the ground filled the temple courtyard.

From the alleys and rooftops, shadows emerged. Naga sadhus, with their well-built bodies and flying dreadlocks, descended upon the invaders. Each Naga warrior knew his share of soldiers to be neutralized. The soldiers had their eyes on their weapons and the Nagas had their eyes on them.

From inside the temple, the priest announced out loud, '*Bali ki prakriya shuru karein* (start the ritual of sacrifice).' He started chanting.

ॐ क्रीं कालिकायै नमः स्वाहा।
Om Kalikaaye Namah Swaha (We offer our salutations
to Goddess Kali; may our offering be pleasing to you).

Ajaa, the leader of the Naga sadhus, moved with a grace and ferocity that seemed otherworldly. His ash-covered body became a blur as he launched himself at the intruders. With a swift manoeuvre, he cut off the head of the soldier who was trying to take a gold necklace off the devi's neck. The man immediately fell to the ground, his blood trickling along the devi's feet.

The priest announced, '*Bali ki prakriya sampann hui* (the ritual of sacrifice has concluded),' and continued his puja as the Nagas continued to fight. His chants boomed throughout the temple. Some Nagas guarded him while Adhiraj kept watch over the weapons so that the Afghan soldiers could not take them back, and had to either surrender or die fighting.

Two soldiers lunged at Narayan, but he sidestepped the attack and threw a spear in the direction of the first soldier, pinning him to the wall. He leapt into the air and using the momentum of his jump, delivered a crushing kick to the second soldier's chest, sending him sprawling.

Realizing the might of Narayan, about ten soldiers attempted to flank him. But, with an uncanny sense of his surroundings, he ducked and rolled, emerging behind them. Soldiers fell with every jab of his dagger. Ajaa ensured that the puja was not stopped at any point, cutting off the hands and legs of any soldier who tried to reach the *garbhagriha*, the innermost sanctum and the most sacred part of the temple.

A group of five soldiers, hoping to overpower Ajaa with numbers, rushed at him. But Shambhu ji intervened and, with his extensive knowledge of hand-to-hand combat, used their group dynamics to his advantage. A push here, a pull there and soon they were colliding with each other, disoriented and vulnerable. He swiftly incapacitated each with chokeholds, joint locks and well-placed strikes.

Ten more soldiers formed a circle around Ajaa, determined to end this whirlwind of death. Ajaa, however, had other plans. Picking up a discarded shield, he used it to deflect incoming attacks, all the while moving closer to his adversaries. Adhiraj also joined him, attacking with his shankh, and with each step, a soldier fell, each death different from the last—a slash across the throat, a dagger to the heart, a broken neck from a well-placed kick.

In mere moments, the Nagas stood in a circle of fallen foes, their eyes burning with a fire fuelled by their love for their goddess. One after another, a mere fifteen Naga sadhus had sent ninety-five Afghan soldiers to their graves.

As the puja concluded, the central hall of the temple rang with the final Sanskrit chants of the sole priest conducting the ritual. The remaining five Afghan soldiers, witnesses to the deadly prowess of the Nagas, felt a fear they had never known and surrendered immediately. The tables had turned. The ambushers were ambushed, and the would-be conquerors of Gokul now faced an uncertain fate.

These five soldiers were taken under the sprawling shade of a banyan tree. It had been there for centuries, silently witnessing countless tales of valour and pain. Today, it bore witness to yet another.

The vast area beneath the tree was crowded with Naga sadhus now, their ash-covered, blood-spattered bodies and fierce demeanours contrasting sharply with the five young, scared and bound soldiers standing in a row. For these Afghan soldiers, the unexpected strength and number of the Naga sadhus was bewildering. They had prepared for a raid on a defenceless village, not a confrontation with such relentless warriors.

Tariq and Farid also stood among the five soldiers, alive. The Naga sadhu who had listened in on their conversation the previous night came up to them and repeated Tariq's exact words, mocking them both.

'Look at them! Playing with ash while we prepare for war. These naked, defenceless nomads are no threat.'

'If they are lucky, they will be gone tomorrow before we raid the town, and if not, they will run with their tails between their legs at simply seeing our weapons.'

'Our hundred Afghan warriors can raze this village to the ground in hours. This town stands as a beautiful, defenceless woman waiting to be claimed by force.' Tariq and Farid, confident that they were alone the previous night, were in shock, wondering how the Naga knew their conversation.

The five soldiers stood in front of the Nagas, unarmed and hands tied. 'You dumb, brainless, foolish men. Sardar Khan will kill all you naked bastards before you can utter the name of your useless gods,' screamed an Afghan survivor.

Ajaa picked up a sword from the pile of weapons on the floor and slashed the commander into two halves before anyone could anticipate his move.

He addressed the soldiers. 'If anybody has something to say, any threat or warning to convey on behalf of Sardar Khan, the sword in my hand is listening.'

Ajaa turned to his fellow sadhus and said, 'I've made my decision. We must send these four soldiers back alive.'

Just then, Narayan sprang to his feet. His voice was filled with anger. 'Ajaa! Why would you spare those who have come to our land with intentions of destruction and death?'

Ajaa met Narayan's gaze. In his calm yet authoritative voice, he said, 'Look at them, Narayan. They aren't seasoned warriors. They are young boys thrust into the face of danger by circumstances we do not know. They are too young to die now . . .'

Narayan, filled with the passion for protecting his people and homeland, was about to retaliate. Just then, the Mathadhish interjected with a calming gesture, 'Narayan, we must trust Ajaa's judgement.'

Narayan, although not in agreement with Ajaa's decision, decided not to pursue the matter further.

The three soldiers, including Tariq and Farid, were then ordered by Ajaa to load the dead bodies of their comrades into the very same horse carriages and bullock carts they had brought to loot the wealth of the temples in Gokul.

As everyone watched this small convoy ride away, a few Naga sadhus seemed restless. Among them was Narayan, who once again got up to air his concerns. His eyes searched for Ajaa's, seeking answers. 'Ajaa, we must be prepared. How many enemies are we up against?'

Ajaa looked out into the distance, his voice steady and calm, 'Narayan, it's not the numbers that should concern us. Our spirit will determine our fate.'

Narayan continued, 'But Ajaa, you have sent those soldiers to warn Sardar Khan, and a much bigger war now awaits us. How will we face this mighty army without weapons?'

Ajaa looked into Narayan's eyes and addressing every Naga present there, he said, 'The Afghans attacked Gokul because it has many temples, but Sardar Khan got the reasoning wrong. Our temples do not contain gold and silver, our temples house armed gods and goddesses. Each and every goddess and god of ours holds deadly weapons. The divine arms that our gods and goddesses wield aren't mere symbols; they are a testament to the might we can harness. Lord Shiva's trishul symbolizes the trinity of creation, preservation and destruction; Lord Vishnu's chakra is symbolic of the endless cycle of time; Maa Durga's sword represents knowledge and power; while goddess Kali is the face of wrath.

'With these weapons, which have been bestowed with divine energies for millennia, and the burning spirit of the Naga sadhus, no force on earth can stand against us. Sardar Khan wants to raid Gokul because there are numerous temples. Go inside these temples and with all due respect borrow weapons from your gods, take their blessings and prepare for victory.'

Adhiraj bowed his head in admiration and pride. The entire assembly seemed awakened and equipped to embrace their destiny, no matter the challenges ahead.

Determination was evident in Shambhu ji's voice when he said, 'Our priority now is to prepare for the impending battle. Sardar Khan's army may be greater in numbers, but we have our strengths and our faith.'

Ajaa added, 'If we prepare strategically, we will be ready to face them in two days.'

The Mathadhish could see the confidence in Ajaa's eyes. He gave a nod of approval. 'Very well, Ajaa, we place our trust in you and the divine guidance of Lord Shiva.'

Ajaa now addressed his fellow Nagas, who awaited their leader's next command: 'Every pious ritual starts with the name of Lord Ganesh, and we are starting a war. Let us all together pray to the god of war, Lord Kartikeya, the eldest son of Lord Shiva, and Lord Ganesh. Har Har Mahadev!'

As Gokul echoed with the roars of 'Har Har Mahadev', an elephant added its trumpet to the call, surprising all the Nagas. Looking in the direction of the sound, the Nagas found Vanraaj shushing Dulari. Tagging along with Dulari and Vanraaj was Golu, who continued his cute trumpeting, circling his trunk even after everybody was silent.

Narayan seemed unimpressed by the arrival of the uninvited Vanraaj. 'I told him not to come, but look, he is here now,' he said in a high-pitched voice. Ajaa looked Narayan in the eyes and turned back to Vanraaj. Narayan had received his answer.

Defusing the tension, Ajaa walked to Vanraaj. Vanraaj bowed respectfully in response.

'What are you doing here? What do you want?' questioned Ajaa.

'We just want to help. I promise that we will be of use,' requested Vanraaj.

'If I let you step into the battle, then I will be in the wrong, as you are not one of us and I can't allow you to risk your life for our cause and purpose. And if I stop you from protecting the people, then that will go against the Nagas' resolve and our dharma. I will allow you to help only if you promise me that you will help us in preparing for the battle, but will leave before the battle starts,' said Ajaa in a firm voice, demanding the answer he needed.

Vanraaj smiled, bowed his head again and agreed to Ajaa's terms.

Ajaa turned to the rest of the group and said, 'In two days, we will face our first battle. It's not just about protecting Gokul, but about our very existence and sacred beliefs. I need every one of you to rally your groups, to prepare mentally and physically.'

A unanimous nod from the leaders and a roaring chant filled the air, joined with the trumpeting of Dulari and Golu, again moving his little trunk, signalling the group's unity and readiness. The stage was set for a confrontation that would forever be immortalized in the chronicles of history.

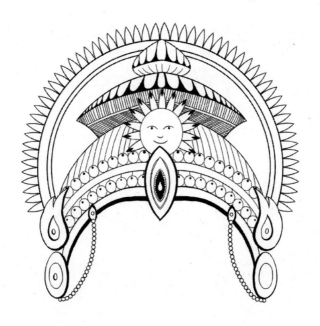

9

A Clear Message

In the grand hall of Haripur, King Vedant paced back and forth, his brow furrowed in deep thought. The golden throne behind him stood vacant, reflecting the ambient glow of the many torches that illuminated the room. The high arches and intricate carvings whispered tales of past glories, but the present seemed uncertain.

His minister, an elderly man with a bald head and no facial hair, broke the silence: 'Maharaj, we have news from our scouts that Sardar Khan is on his way to attack Haripur. They have already started looting and attacking the smaller towns and villages on their way. We need to prepare for war.'

The commander-in-chief, Krishna, said, 'My lord, hindsight is always clearer. All we can do now is prepare and rally our forces. And remember, even in our darkest hour, the spirits of our ancestors and martyrs and the legacy of your father will guide us.' His words comforted the young king.

Yet, Vedant could feel the panic of the upcoming war creeping up on him. 'Sardar Khan cannot go against the orders of Jugal Kishore. There must be some misunderstanding. Send two messengers to Sardar Khan immediately along with the treaty between Jugal Kishore and us,' he commanded them. 'I need to stop this battle at all costs!'

Meanwhile, in Sardar Khan's camp, the partying continued in full swing, celebrating the triumph over Vijaygarh. Tents were decorated with colourful banners and the rhythmic beat of the dhol filled the air. Soldiers danced jubilantly, their faces lit by the warm glow of torches. Flames from large bonfires leapt up, casting flickering shadows on the camp's periphery. The aroma of roasted meat wafted through the air, mingling with the sweet scent of fresh fruit and wine. Musicians played traditional tunes while other performing artists entertained with their antics. Everywhere one looked, there were scenes of indulgence, from games to soldiers sharing tales of loot and murder.

As darkness enveloped the camp, the anticipation of the return of the soldiers from Gokul grew palpable. Sardar Khan sat and waited patiently in his lavishly decorated tent, the soft glow of lanterns revealing the gleam of greed in his eyes. He had already imagined the mountains of gold and treasures the soldiers would bring back.

A sentinel rushed in, announcing the return of the men from Gokul. Unable to contain his excitement, Sardar Khan walked to the entrance, expecting to see carriages overflowing with riches. What met his eyes was a grim spectacle.

Only four soldiers, beaten and tired, walked hesitantly towards him. Their hands were empty; they were terrified. The carriages and carts that should have been weighed down with gold and precious artefacts from Gokul were instead carrying the lifeless bodies of their comrades.

Sardar Khan's delight turned to fury. His face turned a shade darker, his eyes narrowing to dangerous slits. 'Who did this?' he thundered, his voice echoing ominously in the silent camp. The soldiers trembled, the weight of their failure pressing heavily upon them.

'A group of Naga sadhus, led by a Naga named Ajaa,' replied Farid.

Sardar Khan's towering presence dominated the tent as he glared at the soldiers, demanding an explanation. 'Speak! What transpired in Gokul?'

Farid hesitated for a moment before mustering the courage to speak. His voice quivered, 'We underestimated them, my lord. Gokul was not what we expected.'

Sardar Khan's patience was wearing thin. 'Explain!'

Tariq took a deep breath and began, 'It was Ajaa, the leader of the Naga sadhus, along with a few others. We never imagined . . . never believed that any human could possess such skill.'

Farid interjected, 'Their movements were lightning-fast, like a blur. We had no chance. Those ten took down ninety-seven of our comrades, and each move . . . each kill was unique, as if they were born with weapons in their hands.'

Every compliment they paid the Naga sadhu was a blow to Sardar's pride.

Tariq, eyes wide, added, 'It wasn't just their combat skills, my lord. The strength they displayed was otherworldly. They picked up soldiers as if they were mere playthings, tossing them aside.'

'There was a fire in their eyes,' Farid whispered, almost to himself.

Tariq stammered, 'And . . . and there were more like them, all armed, all ready and all waiting for us.'

Sardar Khan, though shaken by the soldiers' tales, masked his unease. 'And you bring me this news? After all our victories?'

The defeated soldiers lowered their heads in shame, the weight of their defeat evident. They had encountered something they were unprepared for.

As Sardar Khan was about to announce their punishment, the tent flaps were pushed aside and two men of regal bearing walked in, accompanied by one of his commanders.

The soldiers instantly straightened their backs and an uneasy silence enveloped the tent.

'Huzoor!' his commander announced, 'these are messengers from Haripur.'

Sardar Khan's annoyance subsided as he took note of the significance of the situation. 'Welcome,' he said with a forced smile, indicating the lavish cushions for them to sit on. Servants quickly presented a tray laden with roasted meat and wine.

The senior messenger eyed the meat and then politely declined, 'We are vegetarians.'

Sardar Khan raised an eyebrow, his smile deepening into an amused smirk. 'A matter of principle or faith?'

'Both,' the same man responded confidently.

Sardar Khan chuckled, 'Very well.' Leaning forward, he continued, 'To what do I owe this visit?'

The senior messenger carefully unrolled a thick parchment scroll sealed with the emblem of Haripur. He handed it to Sardar Khan and said, 'A message from our King Vedant.'

Sardar Khan's fingers gently broke the seal, his eyes scanning the script. As his eyes darted over the scroll, they narrowed with every line he read. The script was clear and the stamp even clearer—the mark of Ahmad Shah Abdali. A treaty between Vedant and Jugal Kishore.

His grip on the parchment tightened, crinkling its edges. The subtle shift in Sardar Khan's demeanour did not go unnoticed. Everyone waited with bated breath for his response.

However, before Sardar could react, the senior messenger pulled out another scroll, clearing his throat before he began reading aloud.

'In the name of peace and prosperity,' he began, his voice unwavering and strong, 'King Vedant of Haripur extends his greetings to Sardar Khan of the Afghan lands. With the blessings and stamp of Ahmad Shah Abdali, this message serves to remind Sardar Khan that a treaty of non-aggression exists between Haripur and the Afghan empire. We hope this treaty stands as a testament to our commitment to peace and mutual respect. Haripur, under the rule of King Vedant, is no enemy of Sardar Khan. Attack Haripur, and it would be seen as overruling Ahmad Shah Abdali himself.'

Sardar Khan's ambition had been thwarted by a piece of parchment. He leaned back, his fingers drumming a thoughtful rhythm on the armrest of his chair, his next move on his mind.

Every soldier and servant within Sardar Khan's vicinity could sense the rage building inside him, a storm ready to be unleashed.

'Anything you'd like to add?' Sardar Khan asked, looking at the junior messenger, his voice dripping with menace. The junior messenger merely shook his head, trying his best to remain composed.

Without warning, Sardar Khan lunged at the junior messenger, forcing him closer. He signalled to one of his men, who promptly handed him a large piece of meat. With a wicked smile, he jammed the leg piece into the young messenger's mouth. The junior choked and gasped, tears streaming from his eyes at his humiliation.

The senior messenger, despite his evident fear, tried to intervene, to spare his companion any further suffering. 'Sardar Khan, we are but messengers and messengers are never harmed!' he retaliated. But Sardar Khan had no intention of listening.

His focus now turned to the senior. With a sinister shine in his eye, he snatched the treaty scroll from the senior messenger's hands, the very paper that had thwarted his ambitions.

'Since the words of this treaty reached me through your mouth . . . I want you to take your words back. Have it as your last meal,' he sneered. With the help of his men, he forced open the man's mouth and brutally thrust the scroll down the senior messenger's throat. The messenger's eyes widened in terror, his muffled cries echoing in the silent tent.

Sardar Khan then took a flask of oil from a nearby table and, with a sadistic grin, poured it on the scroll that eventually flowed into the messenger's throat. Taking a torch, he brought the flame close and, with a swift motion, set the oil alight. The messenger's body jerked violently, his screams silenced by the flames burning his tongue and throat alive, finally consuming him.

The tent was soon filled with a thick, acrid smoke and the nauseating smell of burning flesh. The remaining soldiers and the junior messenger could only watch in horror, struck mute by the barbaric display of power and cruelty. Sardar Khan's message was clear: no parchment, treaty or king would stand in the way of his ambition.

Khan's wrath continued to spill over. The wounded soldiers from the Gokul skirmish, despite their pleas for mercy, were met with only cold rage. Farid, Tariq and the other young soldiers were dragged to the centre of the tent, their fear palpable.

'Did I not train you as warriors? Did I not feed you, clothe you, give you a purpose?' Sardar Khan's voice roared, echoing through the tent. 'And this is how you repay me? With defeat and shame?'

Farid tried to speak, his voice quivering, 'We were ambushed, caught off guard by the sheer strength of the Naga sadhus . . .'

But before he could finish, Sardar Khan signalled to one of his men, and a blade swiftly ended Farid's pleas. One by one, the other two met their grim fate, their lives snuffed out as a clear message of the price of failure. The junior messenger helplessly witnessed the blood and fire, with the meat still in his mouth.

Then, with the tent floor stained with blood, Sardar Khan's gaze shifted to his other commanders and soldiers. 'Has anyone handed you a treaty today? One bearing official stamps and seals?' he asked. The men, knowing the consequences of any wrong answer, quickly shook their heads. Each one avoided Sardar Khan's gaze, hoping not to become the next target of his fury.

His menacing eyes settled on the junior messenger, who was trembling with fear. 'And you? Have you seen such a treaty before?'

The junior messenger, his voice barely audible, stuttered, 'N . . . no, I have not.'

Sardar Khan, taking a deep breath, appeared to calm down, though the air of the tent was still full of the stench of burning human flesh. The cruel display had served its purpose. Everyone present knew the deadly consequences of failure or deception. The night's events had sealed Sardar Khan's reputation as a leader to be both followed and feared.

The junior messenger, still visibly shaken by the horrors he had just witnessed, looked up into Sardar Khan's cold eyes. Sardar, in a tone that left no room for questions, said, 'Go back to your master. Tell him that while he may not consider me an enemy, he should not make the mistake of considering me a friend either. I am neither anyone's servant nor their ally.'

The messenger nodded hurriedly. As he turned to leave, Sardar added, 'And make sure he understands this well: while treaties might bind others, they don't bind me.'

With that, the messenger was quickly escorted out of the tent, carrying a heavy message that would surely resonate in the court of Haripur.

Sardar Khan's attention now turned to his commander. 'How many Naga sadhus are in Gokul right now?' he asked.

'There are around 100 men, said these four cowards before being brought to you,' replied the commander. The estimation was quite close as the total strength of the Nagas, including Ajaa, was 111.

Back in Gokul, Ajaa spoke with determination. 'Dhruv, tell me, what did you see in Sardar Khan's camp? What was the total strength of these soldiers? We must prepare to fight every last one of them.'

'Their numbers are in the thousands,' replied Dhruv.

10

Gokul Is Ready

As dawn broke, Gokul was bathed in a golden hue. But this wasn't just any regular morning. An atmosphere of urgency enveloped the village. Naga sadhus, with their unwavering focus, began gathering weapons from the various temples. Adhiraj blew the shankh, a rallying call for preparation.

Word had spread swiftly, and the locals were gathering in support. Village farmers, with the dust of the fields still fresh on their clothes, hurriedly offered their tools. The axes that had once cut trees were now being offered to protect the village. Large sickles, usually reserved for cutting grass, gleamed menacingly in the sunlight, ready for a new purpose. In the heart of the village, women from various households, their faces lined with fear and determination, amassed a collection of sharp knives, ready to be handed to those who would stand guard.

Shambhu ji, with his gentle presence, meandered through the village, observing the flurry of activity with quiet admiration. Everywhere he went, his eyes scanned the situation, identifying where his expertise and assistance were most needed. At one point, he knelt by a group of farmers, showing them the precise angle at which to sharpen the arrows they were preparing for the sadhus, and the right length and weight required for the arrow to achieve maximum flight and distance. Next, he was with a man, providing his strong arms to help him carry heavy knives and farming tools to the village centre.

In the sadhvis' camp, Dhruv awoke and rose painfully from his bed. His movements made it clear that he had not yet recovered fully. Seeing Shambhu ji just a few steps away, Dhruv mustered the strength to walk to him. Shambhu ji knew without turning that Dhruv was approaching and he spoke: 'Our rich history speaks of the eternal battle between good and evil, young one. While you might not see the full picture now, remember that this fight is to ensure that the light of dharma continues to shine brightly.' Shambhu ji asked Dhruv to follow him. They walked to Adhiraj who had spread out an impressive collection of divine weapons on a large cloth under the shade of a massive peepal tree. When they reached the site, Shambhu ji lifted each weapon with admiration.

First, he picked up the trishul, its three prongs glistening in the sunlight. Shambhu ji began, 'I need not tell you that this belongs to the mighty Lord Shiva. The trishul isn't just a weapon; its three points represent the balance of creation, preservation and destruction. In the hands of Shiva, it reminds us of the cyclical nature of existence, the essence of life and how everything is interconnected.

'In primordial times, when the universe was still taking shape, the devas and asuras were always in conflict. Finally, to obtain the nectar of immortality (Amrita), the devas and asuras decided to churn the cosmic ocean of milk together. This event became known as the Samudra Manthan. While churning the ocean, which they did using Mount Mandar as the pivot and the serpent Vasuki as a churning rope, several divine objects, beings and poisons, emerged. One of the first things to come out was the deadly poison called Halahala. Its fumes started to destroy creation and neither the devas nor the asuras knew how to handle it.

'Witnessing the potential annihilation of creation, the devas sought the intervention of Lord Shiva. In his infinite compassion, Lord Shiva drank the Halahala. While the poison didn't harm Shiva, it turned his throat blue, earning him the name "Neelkantha" or "The Blue-Throated One".

'To neutralize the intense energy of the poison, Shiva needed a weapon of immense power. It is said that the universe itself, recognizing his need, forged the trishul from its elements. The trishul given to Shiva symbolized his control over creation, preservation and destruction—the three functions of the cosmos.

'From that moment on, the trishul became an extension of Lord Shiva, representing his energy and power. It symbolizes his mastery over the three realms: the physical, the metaphysical and the spiritual.

'In various scriptures, Lord Shiva is described using the trishul to restore balance to the universe, ward off evil and uphold dharma.'

Setting the trishul down, Shambhu's fingers grazed the intricate string of a bow. 'In the ancient kingdom of Mithila, a grand *swayamvara* was held for Princess Sita. Suitors from across the land gathered for a chance to win her hand in marriage. The condition was simple but daunting: to lift and string the divine Shiva Dhanush, the sacred bow of Lord Shiva.

'One by one, powerful princes and warriors attempted to lift the bow, but it remained unyielding. Even Ravana tried his hand but couldn't lift it. Then, Lord Rama, the prince of Ayodhya and an incarnation of Lord Vishnu, gracefully stepped forward. With immense strength, he not only lifted the Shiva Dhanush but also effortlessly strung it. The bow, under Rama's divine touch, broke with a resounding crack, filling the hall with astonishment.

'While this feat awed many, it deeply angered Parashuram, the sixth incarnation of Lord Vishnu and a devotee of Lord Shiva. He considered the Shiva Dhanush sacred and was infuriated by its shattering. Determined to understand this act, Parashuram journeyed to the sacred abode of Lord Shiva, Mount Kailash. He confronted the divine deity and demanded an explanation: "How could a mortal, Rama, break your divine bow, the Shiva Dhanush?"

'Lord Shiva calmly explained that events had unfolded according to the grand design of the universe, a part of destiny. Hearing this, Parashuram's anger subsided, and he understood the divine nature of the events.

'As a symbol of reconciliation and goodwill, Lord Shiva, ever compassionate, gifted Parashuram a divine bow, the Vijaya Dhanush, representing Lord Shiva's blessings and forgiveness. With gratitude in his heart, Parashuram accepted the Vijaya Dhanush and the tension that had briefly flared between the two divine beings was replaced by harmony. This remarkable story underlines the intricate relationships within Hindu history.'

Shambhu ji's fingers then moved to the Sudarshan Chakra. 'This weapon is associated with Lord Krishna. It is said to have been crafted by the cosmic architect Vishwakarma, the deity of all craftspeople and architects.

'Vishwakarma once approached Lord Surya (the sun god), to reduce his radiance and heat as it was unbearable. Lord Surya agreed to reduce his heat to benefit the world. Vishwakarma then used the sun's discarded solar essence to forge several divine weapons and among them was the Sudarshan Chakra. He gifted this powerful discus to Lord Vishnu.

'The Sudarshan Chakra, once acquired by Lord Vishnu, became his primary weapon and served as an instrument to restore dharma (righteousness) and dispel adharma (unrighteousness). It's believed that the chakra has the power to annihilate enemies and obliterate evil with precision and speed, always returning to its master after fulfilling its objective. The Sudarshan Chakra was wielded by Lord Krishna, as he is Lord Vishnu's avatar.

Lord Krishna used this weapon for various purposes in his lifetime.

'One such instance has to do with a man named Shishupala, who was the ruler of the Chedi kingdom and a cousin of Lord Krishna. However, instead of sharing a bond of kinship, there was animosity between them. A prophecy had foretold that Shishupala would meet his end at Krishna's hands. Shishupala's mother pleaded with Krishna to forgive her son's offenses. Krishna, always benevolent, promised that he would forgive Shishupala's transgressions, but only up to a limit: a hundred offences.

'The climactic moment came during the grand Rajasuya Yagna organized by the Pandava king Yudhishthira. During the ceremony, they decided to offer Krishna the first worship, as he was deemed the most revered guest. This deeply enraged Shishupala, who was already nursing a grudge against Krishna. He stood up and began insulting Krishna, pointing out every flaw and fabricated tale he could muster, berating him in front of the assembly.

'With every insult, Shishupala unknowingly neared his limit. As he reached the hundredth offence, Krishna's patience ran out. Calmly, without any visible anger, Krishna invoked his Sudarshan Chakra.

'The wheel of fire and energy sprang to life, whirling around before zooming towards the insolent king. In a flash, Shishupala was decapitated, and his life ended as the prophecy had foretold.

'The assembly was stunned into silence. The Sudarshan Chakra, having done its duty, returned to its master. This incident not only showcased the might of the Sudarshan Chakra, but also the boundless patience of Lord Krishna and the inevitability of divine justice.

'Lord Krishna defeated many demons, including Kansa, Shishupala and Jarasandha, using his chakra. Lord Narasimha used his divine chakra to defeat the demon Hiranyakashipu, who could not be killed by man or beast. Lord Vishnu used his Sudarshan Chakra to defeat demons like Rahu, Jayadratha and Hayagriva.

'But it was not only Vishnu's chakra that separated heads from bodies. Our goddesses have also cut heads with swords.' Shambhu ji reached out to stroke a sharp-edged, curved sword that evoked a slight shiver in him. 'This,' he said in a grave voice, 'is the tool of Goddess Durga, especially in her Kaali and Durga avatar. The sword symbolizes divine knowledge, which cuts through ignorance. You will notice that Maa Kaali is always holding a severed head. The severed head represents the ego, which, when unchecked, can lead us astray. Kaali teaches us that sometimes, to find peace and purity, we must face and conquer our inner demons.'

Dhruv's eyes wide with wonder, absorbed Shambhu ji's words, looking at the weapons not just as tools of war but as instruments of wisdom. The tales weren't just of battles and conquests but also of virtues, values and life's profound truths.

Narayan and Ajaa, looking up from their work, smiled realizing that through stories, Shambhu ji was forging a bridge between the past and the present, ensuring that the essence of their dharma would live on in young hearts like Dhruv's.

At the base of the mountain, hordes of Naga warriors worked diligently, pushing massive boulders. Their muscles strained under the weight, determination etched on their faces. The very earth seemed to rumble as the rocks were manoeuvred into position.

Vanraaj also contributed with the help of his majestic elephant Dulari while the little Golu followed his mother everywhere. The magnificent beast, her trumpeting echoing throughout the valley, hauled large logs and stacks of dried grass. Her strength and cooperation were instrumental in the preparations.

The pathway leading to Gokul was a hive of activity. With every passing moment, the Nagas added layers to their defences. Grass, carried in large bundles by the warriors, was laid out meticulously along the route. It wasn't just any grass, but the driest they could find. Vats of flammable oil were brought. With great care, the Nagas spilled it over the grass and the pathway, its pungent aroma mingling with the earthy scent of the surroundings. The oil glistened under the sun, waiting for a spark to unleash its fiery potential.

Between other tasks, Vanraaj and a few Nagas carefully positioned logs, using them to erect barricades and choke points. These would funnel the enemy into the path they desired, making them vulnerable to the traps they had set.

The final touch was camouflage. Using the grass and additional foliage, the Nagas concealed their traps, ensuring that Sardar Khan's advancing army would remain oblivious until it was too late for them.

As the preparations neared completion, a sense of unity and determination permeated the air. The Nagas, with their unwavering spirit and the fruits of their labour before them, stood ready to defend their home against any threat.

Suddenly, the Mathadhish made an announcement meant for every Naga sadhu: 'Assemble! We are having a competition.'

Every Naga sadhu heard the order and arrived to see what the competition was about.

The Mathadhish spoke again, 'A test of speed and endurance will determine the fastest among the Naga sadhus.' As every Naga sadhu started falling in line, another announcement came from the Mathadhish, prohibiting all the seniors, like Ajaa, Narayan and Shambhu ji, from participating. Vanraaj innocently came forward, asking if he could try competing with the Nagas. Vanraaj hoped for a yes but ended up disappointed with the Mathadhish's no. The Mathadhish continued, 'For all those who have qualified on the basis of age and strength, here is the challenge! On the other side, obstructing your path, stand other experienced and stronger Nagas. Some will attack you with fake arrows from a distance, others will try to slow your speed with their physical prowess and fake weapons. Speed is not all you need to win this race; you have to be alert, and your reflexes have to be ready to dodge the arrows and men trying to stop you. The one who reaches Ajaa on the other side will be the chosen one.'

The Mathadhish turned to Ajaa and instructed him to conduct this race, understanding the criticality of speed in unforeseen challenges.

The air was thrumming with anticipation as seventy young Naga sadhus, with their dreadlocks flowing freely, assembled at the starting line. They were a formidable sight, each one a seasoned warrior, honed through years of rigorous training and discipline.

Ajaa, with a stern yet encouraging gaze, surveyed the group. He knew the importance of this moment, the implications it held for the future. In a loud and clear voice, the Mathadhish signalled the start of the race, and like a herd of wild cheetahs unleashed, the sadhus took off.

The race was tough and it was the test of their strength. It was a true trial of their resilience. The track was full of dangers with unbearable heat, which made it even harder to run barefoot. Despite this, they ran with determination, like cheetahs. Some took the hit of fake arrows and many were felled by the barricades. To the villagers and Vanraaj, the scene resembled a battle rather than a race—spine-breaking and punishing, a true test of their spirit. The track was treacherous and filled with obstacles. The ground was melting with heat as they ran barefoot around many hurdles. Their feet were barely touching the ground and their breaths were synchronized with the pounding of their hearts. They were not just running; they were unleashing the power and fury that lay within.

As the dust settled, the last of the runners crossed the finish line. Ajaa, with keen eyes and a swift stride, approached the front-runners. Ten sadhus stood before him, chests heaving, yet eyes blazing with an untamed fire.

With a nod of approval and a sense of pride swelling in his chest, Ajaa declared, 'You were the fastest, the ones who rose above the rest. You are the chosen ones, the Cheetah Dasta. You carry not just the speed, but the strength and spirit of the Naga warriors. The three best among you are Namah, Bhola and Shivay for being the undisputed fastest. Be ready, for you will be summoned when the time is right.' And thus the Cheetah Dasta was formed, an elite unit within the Naga sadhus, swift as the wind and deadly as a storm.

The hiker interrupted, 'Why Cheetah?'

The nameless Naga explained, 'The cheetah is the fastest among all land animals. A cheetah is around 2.7 times faster than humans and can reach speeds of 120 kilometres per hour. The cheetah's rapid acceleration allows it to quickly close the gap and catch its prey.' The hiker asked again, 'But why this race?' The Naga smiled and replied, 'Be patient! Time will tell.'

Meanwhile, a lone messenger made his way back to Haripur to deliver Sardar Khan's ghastly message to King Vedant.

11

Armies on the Move

Vedant's junior messenger, who had barely escaped death
in Sardar's camp, was escorted into the court with the help
of two more men. He looked completely battered and
bruised, his clothes still dusty from the perilous journey.
The trauma of Sardar Khan's actions was evident in his eyes
as he recounted the horrifying event with the scroll.

Vedant listened with mounting dread, his fingers
anxiously tapping the armrest of his throne. The soft glow
of lamps cast shifting shadows across the room, and the air
was heavy with tension.

When Vedant thought the messenger had finished, he
turned to his commander-in-chief, Krishna. However, the
messenger had more to add.

'My king, I need to inform you that there is going to
be another battle before Sardar's army reaches us. They are
headed to Gokul, where a small group of Nagas awaits. It is
my understanding that Sardar is heavily invested in beating

the Naga sadhus in Gokul and until he accomplishes that feat, it will remain his priority.'

Vedant mourned, 'If only we had joined forces with King Manohar. Together, our combined strength would have been formidable. We could've repelled Sardar Khan.'

Krishna nodded in agreement. 'Your father always believed in unity. He always said that it was our strength and our shield against any enemy.'

Vedant's face darkened with regret. 'I should have heeded your advice earlier. I let the honeyed words of Jugal Kishore cloud my judgement.'

'Maharaj, we have allies in places we might not expect. The Naga sadhus in Gokul are not just simple ascetics. They are warriors, bound by their devotion and disciplined training,' said Krishna. Another mantri chimed in, 'Yes, my lord. I've heard tales of their valour and unmatched combat skills. Their leader, Ajaa, is especially renowned. They might be our best bet against Sardar Khan's army.'

Young King Vedant looked up, his eyes showing a glimmer of hope. 'Do they have enough numbers to counter Sardar Khan's forces?'

The commander-in-chief replied, 'On their own, perhaps not. But with our aid and manpower, they can become a formidable force. Their knowledge of the terrain and their guerrilla tactics, combined with our trained soldiers, could turn the tide.'

Vedant took a moment to process this. He knew allying with the Naga sadhus was unorthodox, but desperate times called for desperate measures. And so he decided to form an alliance with the Naga sadhus.

King Vedant made a decision that surprised many in his court; to take the offensive rather than passively wait for the inevitable clash with Sardar Khan. He gave orders to head towards Gokul immediately. His commander-in-chief had advised this move, suggesting that their best chance lay in aiding Gokul and forming a united front against the invader.

Hundreds of Afghan flags—green, bearing a double-bladed sword embroidered in gold—fluttered in the air, signalling the advancing army's formidable presence. The ground trembled as Sardar Khan's vast army marched on its way to Gokul. Their coordinated steps echoed like rhythmic thunder, which announced their approach from miles away. The gleaming green and black uniforms of the soldiers reflected the early morning sunlight, casting a shimmering glow.

Each warrior was decked in intricate armour, designed not just for protection but also for intimidation. Their helmets bore designs of fierce beasts, and their shields carried emblems that represented Ahmad Shah Abdali's power and legacy. This wasn't just an army; it was a massive, moving fortress of men, a storm of horses and camels, a parade of walking weapons.

War drums punctuated their march as flag-bearers holding high the emblem—a roaring lion on a field of green—led the procession. Archers with their bows strung, cavalry with horses snorting impatiently, foot soldiers wielding spears and swords, all marched with a singular purpose: to claim Gokul for Sardar Khan.

Above them, predatory birds circled, drawn to the massive force and perhaps sensing the impending clash. Every village they passed became eerily silent, its inhabitants hiding and watching with a mix of fear and awe.

Meanwhile, back in Gokul, the news of the approaching army spread like wildfire. Ajaa and the Naga sadhus prepared, knowing that the coming battle would test them like never before. Earlier they had briefly faced Sardar's forces, but now they would face the full might of his army. The village grew tense with anticipation, and Gokul braced itself for what was to come.

The Mathadhish had instructed all Naga sadhus to ensure zero civilian casualties. The evacuation of villagers from Gokul had already started; people were forced to pack up their essential belongings and precious items and say goodbye to their beloved land. Women cried in farewell and neighbours exchanged crucial articles that could help the families survive for a few days at least. Many families refused to move and wanted to fight for their land.

'This is our motherland! How can anyone come and claim it just like that? We were born here, and we shall die here too. We will stay here and fight for our homes till our last breath,' cried a man holding his wife and children close. But Ajaa, Shambhu ji and the Mathadhish convinced all the residents of Gokul to leave with the promise that they would ensure their early return.

The Nagas were in a flurry of activity, assembling their weapons, preparing defences and chanting mantras for the upcoming battle. The scent of valour, sacrifice and determination filled the air.

Amid this whirl of activity, Ajaa's calm voice cut through the noise as he called Shambhu ji's name. Shambhu ji walked to Ajaa and the two had a silent exchange of words, a weighty decision hanging in the balance. No one knew what they were discussing. And then, the conversation ended abruptly. Without further words, Shambhu ji nodded, and within minutes, he was seen leaving the village, accompanied by a small group of elderly Nagas, their once fierce forms now bent with age. All the other Nagas were surprised to see Shambhu ji leaving them all at such a time, when he was needed the most.

'Where are these Nagas going? Why is Shambhu ji leaving with the villagers?' asked some Nagas, approaching Ajaa.

'Because I asked them to. They are old and they will die if not accompanied by the young and powerful.'

These words were a huge disappointment and shock for the Naga warriors.

Vanraaj was still helping along with Dulari and Golu, lifting the villagers' luggage and placing it on their bullock carts. Ajaa approached him. 'Vanraaj! The time has come, my friend. You too are leaving with the villagers.' Seeing his disappointment, Ajaa continued, 'You have been of immense help, Vanraaj. You have played your role beautifully and your contributions will never be forgotten, but it is time for you to leave Gokul.'

'But why, Ajaa? I can fight. I won't go anywhere. There is still much that I can do. You'll see, Ajaa. Please give me a chance!' Vanraaj pleaded, trying to fight Ajaa's decision. But Ajaa was determined.

'Do you remember the promise you made the day you came here?'

'Yes, that I could stay in Gokul but would have to leave whenever you demanded it,' replied Vanraaj with a long face.

In the medical camp, Shambhu ji, before leaving, walked up to Dhruv, who stood waiting for his orders to line up for the battle against the Afghans. He placed a hand on Dhruv's shoulder. 'I don't know if we will meet again, but this, my friend, is a gift from me, towards your new resolve. Rise and raise your *pharsa* against the wrong and fulfil your destiny,' said Shambhu ji as he handed over a razor-sharp axe to Dhruv. Dhruv bowed and, with both hands, accepted the weapon.

Whispers of Shambhu ji leaving spread like wildfire. The Nagas halted their activity, their eyes following the departing group, a mix of confusion and anger etched on their faces. Some saw it as a betrayal, others as Ajaa's favouritism towards Shambhu ji . The murmurs grew louder and the atmosphere grew tense. A few of them insisted that Narayan raise the issue with Ajaa.

'Ajaa, why did you allow Shambhu ji to leave us at a time when we need him the most? Is your heart softened towards your guru? Is his life more precious than ours?' asked Narayan.

Ajaa, seeing the collective unrest, climbed atop a raised platform. 'Brothers,' he began, his voice echoing across the camp, 'I understand your concerns, your doubts.

'There are only two options. Either you trust me and fight with me or you don't trust me and don't stand by my side. It's still not late. I trust you all, and I stand my ground. Now the choice is yours. I would gladly lay down my life for any of you, and I know all who stay would do the same for me. But this is not about individual lives. This is about our collective future. I decide not for Shambhu ji or me. I decide for us. I have decided what I felt was best . . . It's your turn to take your best decision.'

The Nagas exchanged glances. The Mathadhish took a few steps forward and said, 'I trust you, and I stand with you unconditionally.' The murmurs slowly ceased, replaced by a renewed focus on the battle at hand. The unity of the Nagas was once again fortified, ready to face whatever challenges lay ahead.

*

Sardar Khan, on the other side, sat atop his imposing steed, surveying the lush landscape before Gokul. The horizon was dotted with the vast spread of his battalion—thousands of armoured soldiers, the shimmer of their weapons visible even from a distance, standing in readiness. An officer galloped up to Sardar Khan, saluting promptly. '*Huzoor*, a few of our scouts haven't returned. They went to inspect the terrain, but there is no sign of them.'

Sardar Khan cast a glance at the officer, a slight smirk playing on his lips. 'Look around you.' He gestured grandly at the vast army that stretched as far as the eye could see. 'Do you really think a few missing men will make any difference?'

The officer lowered his gaze, 'No, Huzoor.'

'Good. Let's proceed,' Sardar Khan commanded, his voice dripping with confidence. In his mind, the conquest of Gokul was already a reality.

The rhythmic march of thousands of feet resonated across the land, like an approaching hurricane, as Sardar Khan's battalion moved closer to Gokul. The stakes were high, but Sardar's confidence was unwavering.

Meanwhile, the missing soldiers from Sardar Khan's army, who had been sent one day earlier to inspect the forward area near Gokul, were standing before Jugal Kishore, recounting what had happened to the Haripur messengers in Sardar Khan's tent.

Jugal Kishore's face, usually calm and composed, had turned a shade darker with every word from his spies. He clenched his fists, veins throbbing on his temples. His association with Sardar Khan was tactical, a means to expand his influence and power. After a seemingly interminable silence, he spoke, his voice cold and measured, 'Sardar Khan has crossed the line. His actions stain our reputation and break the very codes of warfare and diplomacy. We must stop him. We cannot let such contempt go unchecked. We cannot afford to be seen as weak or complicit in Sardar's actions. It's good that he chose to kill those poor Nagas in

Gokul before going to Haripur. We have time to reach him before he attacks King Vedant. We will march for Gokul immediately and stop Sardar Khan before he wreaks further havoc in Haripur. Prepare the army.'

The commander saluted, his determination evident: 'It will be done, my lord.'

As the commander left to rally his forces, Jugal Kishore pondered over the unfolding events. Alignments were shifting. The road to Gokul, it seemed, was becoming the epicentre of a confrontation that would reshape the fate of the entire region.

Back in Gokul, Ajaa looked out at the narrow route that led away from Gokul. Shambhu ji, a few old Nagas and Vanraaj were escorting the people of the city to a safe area. The torchlight highlighted Ajaa's form on the imposing cliff, his Bhagva flag fluttering rebelliously against the night breeze.

Adhiraj walked towards the solitary figure. He could sense the weight on Ajaa's shoulders. In a soft, concerned tone, he said, 'You look lost. You can share your concern with me if it at all comforts you in any way.' Ajaa turned and looked in Adhiraj's eyes as if strengthening his trust in him by understanding the age of his soul. He took a moment and decided to say what he felt.

With a sense of guilt, Ajaa replied, 'Yes, I feel lost. Sometimes, a person knows that nobody can comfort him or solve his problems, but he still just wants someone to hear them because simply saying it aloud is a relief that the burden of pain is shared. I am blessed that I reached here, so close to my Lord Shiva. I have had the privilege of serving him, but this one question makes it all incomplete for me. There are battles that one fights within. I'm suffering from not knowing who I am! Whose son? Whose blood? Whose pride? Whose redemption? I don't want these unanswered questions to pull me back into this immortal world, denying me salvation. This question about my origin has haunted me forever. I asked Shambhu ji and the Mathadhish many times, but they have no answers either. I am ready to leave this world with the identity that I now proudly wear but not with the question about the identity I was born with in this God-land. I know who I am, but I don't know where I came from. I know you can't help me—no one can—but I am grateful that you asked, and I could unburden myself a little one last time.' A smile flickered briefly on Ajaa's face as Adhiraj saw Ajaa's eyes. Ajaa looked at the sky as if asking the stars the same question. Adhiraj felt helpless. He stood by Ajaa's side, gazing at the stars in the night sky.

As the sun began its ascent, in Haripur, the horizon was filled with the silhouettes of Vedant's forces. Elephants, adorned with armoured plates, moved with a stately grace, their tusks gleaming. Cavalry units, their armour polished to a shine, rode alongside the infantry. Flags bearing the emblem of Vedant's kingdom fluttered in the breeze, a vivid testament to his kingdom's might and resolve.

Vedant himself rode at the front, a picture of determination and royalty. He was dressed in golden armour, his helmet adorned with a plume that signalled his status as the king. Beside him rode Krishna, his seasoned commander-in-chief, their discussions echoing the urgency of the situation.

'The Nagas stand no chance against Sardar Khan's army without us. They need us more than we need them. This alliance is our best chance. We must reach Gokul as soon as we can. Only a united front can halt his advance,' Krishna remarked, his voice firm.

Vedant nodded. As the army marched on, the villagers and townsfolk from the regions they passed cheered them on. They had heard tales of Sardar Khan's brutality, and the sight of their king marching to confront this threat brought hope to their hearts. The path to Gokul was fraught with uncertainty, but with Krishna beside King Vedant taking the lead, there was a palpable sense of hope.

There were now three armies approaching Gokul from three different sides and in the centre were less than a hundred Naga warriors, their numbers reduced after Shambhu ji had left with the other old Nagas.

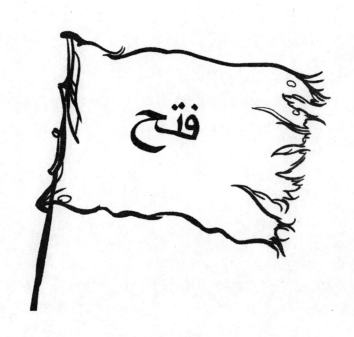

12

The First Wave

The vast, extensive landscape of Gokul was about to become the stage for converging armies soon, each with its own purpose and leader. From the north was approaching the young King Vedant with his army. One day away from the battleground, an impressive spectacle of discipline and power, their march was like the rhythmic dance of war drums. The flag-bearers held aloft banners that fluttered fiercely in the wind, showcasing the emblem of Vedant's kingdom: a majestic lion against a backdrop of golden sun. This was a kingdom known for its valour and resilience, and its march bore testimony to its reputation.

From the east, another force was on the move, a day away from Gokul. Led by Jugal Kishore, trying to cover a comparatively longer distance than the rest, it moved with a more urgent pace, the soldiers' determination evident in every step. Their flags bore the emblem of a soaring falcon; that was another regiment of Ahmed Shah Abdali's unending army, representing their unmatched swiftness and keen vision. Jugal Kishore, having been alerted by the defectors from Sardar Khan's army, knew the stakes and was determined not to let the crazed invader prevail.

Vedant and Jugal Kishore were approaching the same destination from different directions, but with similar goals. Their destinies, it seemed, were intertwining, converging on the battlefield of Gokul, where war was set to begin.

The distant beating of war drums and the faraway roars of the armies reached Dhruv's ears even in the confines of the treatment camp. Lying on the makeshift bed, he felt the ground beneath him vibrate with the force of the battle. He knew this sound from the day of the destruction of his village. The only difference was that last time, the sound had terrified him to death, but now, it was an invitation to kill. His warrior instincts were afire, the adrenaline surging through him with every beat of the drum. He longed to grasp his axe, to stand shoulder to shoulder with Ajaa and the other Naga warriors.

Struggling, Dhruv tried to rise, his gaze instinctively turning towards the battlefield. The fire of determination burnt in his eyes. 'I need to be there,' he rasped out.

A gentle touch on Dhruv's shoulder halted his efforts. It was Shyama, the oldest and the most senior sadhvi at the treatment camp. She had a shaved head and uneven nails cut short as she paid no significance to outer beauty. Her face was stern, the skin bronzed from years of sun exposure, deep wrinkles etched into it that told stories of wisdom and experience. She had piercing slate-grey eyes that seemed to have seen centuries pass, always observing, giving her an air of natural authority. Her hands were strong, with prominent veins and knotted knuckles. These were hands that had both healed and fought. She was more a hammer than a healer.

She signalled to Dhruv to lie back, her eyes caring yet strict. She said, her voice carrying a tone of finality, 'Dhruv, we promised Ajaa we would keep you alive and safe and heal you before this battle ended. Your purpose is different from the purpose of the ones fighting today. You must rest and heal.'

'But my duty is out there!' Dhruv retorted, frustration clear in his voice, his heart heavy with the need to join his comrades.

Adyama, another sadhvi, had accompanied Shyama. The more lenient of the two, she spoke up now. 'If you rush now, injured as you are, you are endangering yourself, Ajaa and all the Nagas. One weak link in the formation is a weak formation for all. The first thing you need to learn is to obey and trust.' Adyama was much younger than Shyama. Slightly shorter, she nevertheless had the aura of Goddess Kali's strength about her. Her skin spoke tales of her years spent as a sanyasin, wandering in scorching heat. She had long, dishevelled dreadlocks flying loose and a particularly sweet, maternal smile.

Dhruv's eyes stung as he held back his tears. Caught between his wish to avenge the children of his village and honouring the promise the sadhvis had made to Ajaa on his behalf, he was lost. Their words made sense, but the heart's yearnings were hard to ignore.

Leaning close, Shyama whispered, trying to soothe Dhruv's agitated spirit, 'Your moment will come, Dhruv. The battle might be upon us today, but there are wars in the future that need your guidance. Trust the path ahead.'

The combat chorus might have been distant, but right there, in the heart of the camp, Dhruv was facing a different kind of battle—a battle of patience, understanding and hope for what lay ahead.

As the first light of dawn broke, the silhouettes of the Naga leaders became starkly visible. Ajaa stood with his formidable trishul, Narayan with his mace and the Mathadhish carried his blade. These mighty figures, backed by their army behind them, seemed to grow in stature, presenting an intimidating front.

On the grounds outside Gokul, death hovered above the living beings waiting for the game of pain to begin. A lone soldier from Sardar Khan's battalion, holding a gleaming brass megaphone, stepped forward. His voice echoed across the valley, carrying a tone of authority, 'Consider this not the first but the last warning! Surrender now and you will be spared. Resist and face the wrath of Sardar Khan!'

Ajaa's response was swift. Raising the Bhagva flag high above his head, he drew a deep breath and bellowed, 'Har Har Mahadev!' The powerful words reverberated throughout the mountains, echoing back from every direction.

From behind him, the Naga warriors, standing tall and defiant, took up the chant. Their voices melded into a thunderous roar: 'Har Har Mahadev!' The sheer volume of their united voices caused the very ground to tremble, sending a wave of energy across the battlefield. Birds took flight and the atmosphere grew thick with anticipation.

Adhiraj stood tall and determined, his fingers wrapped around the shankh. Its rousing call cut through the morning mist and sent chills down the spines of all who heard it.

The atmosphere was electrifying. The pulsating beats mirrored the heartbeats of the warriors, gearing up for the monumental confrontation.

Sardar Khan squinted as figures emerged from the dawn. The Nagas, against the backdrop of the rising sun, appeared surreal. They looked less like men and more like otherworldly beings—fierce, mysterious and powerful. The play of their shadows made them appear like predatory creatures from an ancient world, ready to feast on their prey.

And then, from the Naga ranks, rose a roar. It wasn't the cry of a few hundred men. The noise struck terror into the hearts of many in Sardar Khan's army. They had faced numerous adversaries in their many conquests, but this was unlike anything they had ever encountered. The Nagas were not just defending their homeland, they were fighting for their beliefs, their way of life, and every roar, every beat of the dhol, reinforced their unwavering resolve. It felt to Sardar Khan and his commanders as though these mad nomads were not preparing for war but for worshipping the god of destruction, distributing death as prasad to whoever stepped further.

Sardar Khan, seated on his grand steed, glanced at his chief: 'Are the reports about their numbers correct?'

The chief, equally bewildered by the sheer display of unity and strength, hesitated before replying, 'They don't seem to be.'

The morning light coloured the sky in saffron, the sun yet to show up from behind the mountain. The Nagas were now clearly visible.

Sardar Khan's keen gaze shifted to his battalion of archers. With a brief nod from him, they swiftly took their positions, bows drawn, awaiting the command from their leader.

Each passing second felt like an eternity. The archers' eyes were fixed on the distant figures of the Nagas, calculating trajectories, measuring the wind. And then, with a thundering voice, the commander shouted, 'Aim! Stretch! Release!'

Thousands of arrows ascended in a synchronized dance, their fletchings whistling as they cut through the morning air. It was a breathtaking sight, a proof of Sardar Khan's might and precision.

However, as the arrows approached the intended targets, gravity and the terrain began to play their parts. The elevated cliff on which the Nagas stood acted as a natural shield. Instead of piercing the Nagas, the arrows found their resting place on the ground before them, some embedded in the soft soil, others bouncing harmlessly off rocky outcrops.

Ajaa now held a bow in his hand. 'Brothers, look around you. To your left, to your right. You'll find brethren, comrades, fellow Naga sadhus who have travelled the same arduous path as you. We've undergone the same training, faced the same trials. We've embraced the life chosen for us and renounced worldly pleasures, not as an escape but as a testament to our indomitable spirit.

'Think back to the early days of our journey as Naga sadhus. The rugged terrain we trekked, the mountains we climbed, the rivers we crossed, not merely as tests of physical endurance but of our spiritual mettle. Remember the freezing Himalayan nights when we meditated without flinching, the midday sun under which we trained, preparing not just our bodies but our souls for the battlefields of life?

'Our dreadlocks,' he said, touching his own, 'are not just symbols of renunciation. They are testament to our patience, our commitment. Each strand tells a tale of endurance, of battles fought within and without. Our dreadlocks have seen more sunrises and sunsets than most, and they are prepared to witness many more.'

He swept a hand over his ash-smeared body. 'The ash we wear isn't just from any fire. It is the residue of our past, the very essence of transformation. It reminds us that, just as wood turns to ash, our fears, our hesitations can be incinerated, leaving only courage. With this ash, we wear our resilience, our ability to rise from ruin.' His words breathed motivation into the Nagas, their bodies fuelled with rage.

From his vantage point, Ajaa watched the failed onslaught with a mixture of confidence and aggression. The terrain played the first line of defence for the Naga warriors.

'What are these mad sadhus waiting for?' thought every Afghan soldier, including their commanders.

With the first rays of the sun, Ajaa released the Nagas' first arrow, its clean trajectory piercing the sky. It landed directly in the chest of Sardar Khan's spokesperson, who had warned them to surrender. Sardar Khan and his army could not even see the arrow coming because of the brightness of the sun.

With a steely resolve, Ajaa raised his hand, signalling to his band of Naga archers. Their bows, while fewer in number, were more than just weapons; they were extensions of the Nagas themselves. Each Naga archer closed his eyes briefly, breathing in rhythm with the heartbeat of the earth, feeling the energy around him. Then, on Ajaa's command, all of them released their arrows.

Unlike the mass onslaught of Sardar Khan's troops, the Nagas favoured precision. The green flag fell with the first strike. Each arrow, driven by purpose and skill, found its mark, killing a soldier each with deadly accuracy.

By the time the Afghan soldiers figured out that the Naga warriors were waiting for the sun to blind them, many men were dead.

Sardar Khan's face tightened in frustration. 'Shields up!' he shouted, his voice echoing across the battlefield. The first lot of his soldiers scrambled, large metal and leather shields forming an impenetrable barrier as they advanced.

Sardar Khan's general, realizing the threat the Naga archers posed, shouted, 'Move forward!' The shielded army began its march, making it difficult for the arrows to penetrate its defences.

The rhythmic sound of marching boots mixed with the twang of the Naga bows as arrows continued to rain down. While the shields blocked many, a few found gaps and weak points, underscoring the Nagas' prowess in archery. The battlefield was slowly turning into a tense dance between defence and precision.

Sardar Khan's army marched towards the Naga warriors, keeping an eye up in the clouds for the flying arrows. The landscape ahead appeared smooth, the ground seemingly firm beneath their feet. But as they advanced, a murmur rippled through the first line of soldiers, an unsettling awareness that something wasn't right.

'Hold on! The ground beneath us is collapsing!' cried a soldier in the forefront, his voice tinged with a mixture of shock and panic.

But the momentum of hundreds of advancing soldiers is not easily halted. As the soldier's warning rang out, the ground beneath them collapsed. It was as if the earth itself was swallowing them up. The men fell into the camouflaged trenches and were hit by the spears placed there. Screams rent the air as the sharp edges pierced through heads, chests, stomachs and legs.

'No! Back! Go back!' another line of soldiers yelled, but their cries were barely audible over the clatter of shields, weapons and marching feet. Men screamed in terror as they fell into the concealed trenches. The sharp points of *bhalas* (spears) and iron rods glistened as they pierced through armour and flesh, cruelly claiming life after life. From above, the archers' attack continued, striking whoever moved his eyes from the skies to check the ground beneath his feet.

'Pull me up!' begged a soldier, 'help me,' said another. Hands desperately reached out from the edge of the deadly trenches, blood dripping. But the advance of the army was relentless, and many were trampled in the chaos.

The march didn't stop, and the front lines of Sardar's army fell into the trenches one after the other.

Suddenly, an ominous rumbling echoed from the cliffs surrounding the battlefield. The soldiers glanced upwards just in time to see massive boulders breaking away from the cliff face.

'Rocks! Look out!' screamed a voice.

But the warning came too late. The boulders, powered by both gravity and the deliberate push of Naga warriors, crashed down upon the remaining soldiers. The impact was catastrophic. Armour crumpled under the force, bones shattered and screams were abruptly silenced as the rocks crushed everything in their path. Dust and debris billowed up, creating a thick haze over the scene of devastation.

The marching rhythm of the army, once a unified beat, was now disrupted by panicked shouts. 'Fall back! Retreat!' some cried, while others desperately tried to aid their crushed and maimed companions.

The few soldiers who had somehow managed to cross the traps felt something damp under their feet but in their haste, mistook the oil-soaked grass for dewdrops.

Through the dusty haze, a lone figure could be seen standing tall: Ajaa, with a fire-tipped arrow nocked to his bowstring. Without hesitation, he released the arrow, which soared into the sky like a fiery dragon. As it descended, it ignited the oil-soaked grass.

The fire roared to life in an instant. Those who had survived the fall and the rocks now faced this new, blazing adversary. The flames, orange and red with fury, leapt and danced as they consumed the trenches. Screams of agony pierced the air, mingling with the crackling of the fire.

'Help! Water! Somebody, please!' one soldier cried out, his voice desperate over the roar of the flames.

Another, his leg pinned under a fallen comrade, shouted, 'Don't leave me here! Please!'

The heat was intense, creating a wall of shimmering air between the two opposing forces. The smell of burning flesh, oil and metal filled the air, making it difficult to breathe. The once mighty army of Sardar Khan was now in panic, reeling from the unexpected and masterful tactics of the Naga warriors.

The remaining soldiers, those who had managed to escape the deadly traps, stood paralyzed. The battlefield before them, once a symbol of their expected victory, was now a grim display of death and devastation.

From a distance, faintly audible over the carnage, came the unified chant of the Nagas, a haunting reminder of their power and resilience against their adversaries: 'Har Har Mahadev!'

Almost 250 Afghan soldiers were killed without the Nagas losing even one man.

The sun was now high in the sky, illuminating the field of battle. A landscape once quiet and peaceful was now

painted with the scars of war: smoky fires, fallen soldiers
and crushed armour littered the ground.

Sardar Khan had a grim look of frustration on his face.
The battle was not playing out in his favour. The Nagas,
seemingly the underdogs, were proving to be a force to be
reckoned with.

The air was filled with the twang of bowstrings, the
chants of 'Har Har Mahadev' and the screams of dying
soldiers. Amid this chaotic symphony, an arrow sliced
through the air, aiming straight for Sardar Khan's heart. It
was an incredible shot, one that could only have come from
a master archer. The soldiers closest to Sardar held their
breaths. Time seemed to slow down as the arrow neared
its target.

But with a lightning-fast reflex, Sardar snatched the
arrow from mid-air, mere inches from his chest. His eyes,
burning with fury, locked on to Ajaa, the Naga leader who
stood tall and unyielding on a distant ridge.

A hushed awe fell upon the battlefield. Here were two
leaders, both with incredible skill and fearless determination.
Theirs was a battle of wills as much as it was of armies. Both
sides now recognized that this wasn't just a fight for land or
treasure. It was a fight for honour, legacy and the very soul
of their people.

*

Sardar Khan, gripping his weapon tightly, scanned the field
of carnage with narrowed eyes. The Nagas' unexpected

strategy had put his army on the back foot, and he had to act swiftly to regain the upper hand.

The resilient roars of the Naga warriors echoed through the valley, reminding Sardar that this battle was far from over.

Unaware of the display of the Nagas' valour and Sardar Khan's might, the armies of Jugal Kishore and Vedant were marching towards the land of legends.

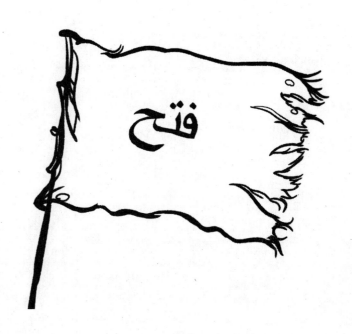

13

The Second Wave

In the cold cave, where the night was getting darker, basking in the warmth of the fire, the curious hiker, Thomas, asked, 'What happened next?' The nameless Naga started to narrate the untold tale of the Nagas, of the feat that changed the fate of Gokul forever.

*

As the winds of destiny blew, Sardar's second lot of soldiers found themselves face-to-face with Ajaa and the Naga warriors. The Nagas were a sight to behold. Adorned in war paint, their bodies smeared with ash, their dreadlocks flying wild, they looked less like men and more like the Veerbhadra Avatar, incarnations of Lord Shiva.

Thomas was confused. 'Veerbhadra Avatar! What's that?'

The nameless Naga started to explain: According to the Shiva Purana, Lord Shiva had nineteen avatars. Veerbhadra was one of the nineteen avatars. Veerbhadra, a fierce avatar, was born from Shiva's anger when his wife, Sati, immolated herself due to her father's disrespect. Veerbhadra was created to avenge Sati's death and punished her father, King Daksha, by beheading him during a grand yajna. To halt the destruction, Shiva intervened to calm Veerbhadra's anger. He did so by performing the Tandava dance and then, through his divine power, resurrected Daksha with a goat's head, symbolizing forgiveness and reconciliation. This act ended Veerbhadra's rampage and restored balance. In Gokul, there was no Lord Shiva to stop the hundreds of Veerbhadras. Chaos and bloodshed were inevitable.

On the battlefield, the Nagas wielded their trishuls, swords, maces and bows with inhuman dedication, their eyes gleaming with a savage intensity. Their war cries echoed across the plains, a haunting chorus that sent shivers down the spines of even the bravest.

The Afghan soldiers, many of whom were veterans of countless battles, felt an unfamiliar sensation—raw, uncontrolled fear. Their faces, usually patient and expressionless, now showed traces of uncertainty and nervousness. Whispers ran through the ranks of those who watched and they exchanged uneasy glances. The legends they had heard about the Naga warriors, which they had dismissed as mere mythology, appeared terrifyingly real.

Each step the Nagas took was heavy and purposeful, making the enemy's heart quiver. Their battle formations were erratic, yet there was an underlying solidity, a unity born out of years of practice and brotherhood.

Sardar's soldiers tried to maintain their discipline, chanting their prayers under their breath and gripping their weapons tighter. The weight of what was to come pressed heavily on their hearts. They were mentally unprepared to face the Nagas. They had never thought that their first line of offence, around 500 soldiers-strong, would turn defensive in fear and would perish in such a manner. They were like dried leaves, ready to fall to a handful of Nagas who had no formations, no shields and no symmetry of weapons.

The fierce sun beat down on the field, creating mirages on the horizon and making it seem as though the army of Sardar Khan was moving on a sea of shimmering waves. This second wave of his soldiers marched in perfect synchronicity, their armour glinting, shields raised and spears pointing forward. They resembled an impervious wall of steel, trained to break through any resistance. But before they could break the temple walls of Gokul, their morale was broken as huge boulders, pushed by some hidden Nagas, hurtled down, crushing a few and blocking the way. The second wave of the Afghan battalion was thus divided into two halves. The first half of these soldiers now had to walk through a living hell—the corpses of their own dead—and face the wrath of the Naga warriors, whereas the other half had to find a way to break the barrier of boulders that was stopping them from helping and saving their own and uniting against the sadhus. The bodies of the Afghans numbered in hundreds. Some had their limbs missing, the skin of some was almost burnt to a crisp and a few had arrows and spears embedded in their bodies. Dead, protruding eyes stared at the living. The visuals were horrifying, even for the demon-like soldiers of Sardar's army.

Yet, their steps remained perfectly coordinated, every soldier precisely where he needed to be. The hum of their collective chant grew louder: 'For Allah, for victory!'

The Nagas, in stark contrast, charged with no formation whatsoever. Some sprinted forward with wild abandon, others sidestepped quickly and dodged, while a few stood their ground, simply waiting for the enemy to come to them. The Afghan soldiers' chorus seemed soft in comparison with the chants of the Nagas: 'For the temples we protect, and the gods we serve!'

'Strike like lightning!' yelled Ajaa, his voice raw from the battle cry, as he lunged forward.

Another young Naga, not far from Ajaa, roared as he ducked under a swinging blade.

'They are asuras and their defeat is certain because the gods fight with us,' Ajaa encouraged his men. Each Naga sadhu killed more than ten Afghan soldiers alone; they were like unstoppable drill machines, no metal too tough for them to penetrate.

Their unstructured assault was like the relentless and overwhelming shore stopping the storm and breaking the waves into mere harmless drops. The Naga warriors seemed to possess an undefeatable energy, a madness that gave them incredible strength and speed. Every Naga was a whirlwind of destruction, their arms moving so fast that they seemed to blur.

'Crush their defences and bones, their formations won't save them today!' Ajaa shouted, swiping his sword through the air and killing three soldiers in swift succession.

The structured formation of Sardar's army disintegrated rapidly. Panic set in as the soldiers found themselves unable to fend off these unpredictable and ferocious attackers. Men fell, some pierced by weapons, others trampled in the chaos.

In the yelling and screaming of the battlefield, Narayan stood out. His ash-smeared body glistened with sweat and blood and in his hands, he held a massive gadaa, which he had borrowed from a large Hanuman statue—an emblem of raw strength. A group of Afghan soldiers, swords drawn, advanced towards him, thinking of overpowering him with sheer numbers.

An Afghan soldier lunged, but Narayan moved like a shadow, swinging the gadaa in a wide arc. The mace's heavy end connected with the soldier's helmet, crushing it and sending him sprawling. Another tried a flank attack, only to be met with the gadaa's shaft, which Narayan used to sweep the soldier's legs from under him.

A duo advanced in coordination, one attacking high and the other low. With a roar, Narayan spun on his heels, using the gadaa's momentum to create a whirlwind of destruction. The one attacking from below got the gadaa's shaft across his face, breaking his nose and knocking out his teeth. The one attacking from above found the gadaa's heavy end smashing into his chest, bones breaking upon impact.

But it wasn't just the gadaa, it was the man wielding it. Narayan's every swing, strike and parry displayed an unmatched mastery of the weapon, turning it into an extension of his own body. The Afghan soldiers had never seen anything like it.

By the time Narayan's dance of death ended, a ring of fallen soldiers surrounded him, a testament to the might of the Naga sadhus and the power of their sacred weapons.

As the fight continued, the battlefield echoed with the metallic clinks of armour and the fierce cries of warriors. 'Jai Bholenath!' screamed Adhiraj. Although he lacked experience, he compensated for it with lots of zeal and speed. A khadag in hand, he charged at the Afghan front, moving with the fury of a tempest. With every step, he thrust the khadag forward, its edge impaling any soldier unfortunate enough to be in his path. 'For Mahadev!' he yelled as three Afghan soldiers tried to flank him, only to be sliced by the blade.

Nearby, Ajaa's hulking figure brandished his trident with unmatched prowess, charging into a group of Afghans. Each swing of his weapon cut through armour and flesh like a hot knife through butter. An enemy soldier tried to stab him from behind, but Ajaa whirled around, the trident's crushing weight smashing the soldier to the ground, helmet and all.

At the other end of the field, the Mathadhish wielded his axe with grace and brutality. With a fierce yell of 'Shambho Shankara!' he swung the battleaxe over his head and brought it down with such force that he beheaded two Afghan soldiers in one swift motion. Seeing a group charging at him, he rotated the axe, its sharp blade singing a deadly lullaby, maiming all who dared approach.

A few metres away from them, Narayana, skilled at mace fighting, danced around his foes with his heavy hanuman weapon. The mace with its metal shine became a blur as he moved. 'Rudra's fury guides us!' he shouted, thrusting the mace forward and crushing an enemy's chest. Blood gushed from the mouths of Afghan soldiers from all sides as he stood between them, bathing in it.

Throughout the battlefield, the Nagas yelled in encouragement, zeal and motivation. Their shared belief was profound, with each of them fiercely defending the others, charging forward and retreating in perfect harmony.

The second wave of Afghan soldiers, initially confident in their numbers, were now retreating in chaos, the ferocity of the Naga sadhus breaking both their ranks and spirit. The Nagas moved like a force of nature, unstoppable, with divine fury driving them. The day seemed destined to be painted in the saffron glory of the Naga sadhus.

By the time dusk began to cast its long shadows on the battlefield, it was evident that the Nagas had gained the upper hand. The Naga warriors gathered, their voices rising in a triumphant chant, 'Har Har Mahadev! The gods are with us!'

14

The Crown and the Prince

In the old times, blowing a shankh at sunset was considered the announcement of the end of fighting for the day, to be resumed the next day at first light. After the evening *shankhnaad*, soldiers from both sides would collect their dead and injured before dark. And so, at the end of the first day's battle, Adhiraj blew the shankh. The day's fighting ceased, and the sun was about to set. It was time for soldiers to pick up their wounded and cremate the dead following the proper rituals, but after experiencing the fierce Nagas, Sardar Khan's soldiers were so terrified that they did not have the courage to collect their wounded fellows. While the soldiers stood at a safe distance, watching their fellow soldiers craving for help, first aid and water, the shadows of the Naga warriors stretched long over the battlefield, casting an eerie darkness on the dead and injured. Finally, it was the Naga sadhus who walked forward, their blood-covered bodies still sparkling with sweat and ash from the day's fight, and began searching among the dead and collecting the wounded Afghan soldiers. The Afghan troops stood on their side of the battlefield helplessly, looking at the Naga warriors roaming free and unbothered among hundreds of corpses, searching for any surviving Afghans, wondering why they were there and what they were searching for when they had no dead warriors in the battlefield.

'Please . . . mercy . . .' screamed a young Afghan soldier to his brothers from afar. His leg was disjointed, eyes wide with fear. Another, clutching a bleeding arm, murmured desperate prayers in agonizing pain, 'Please kill me or save me. Don't leave me here.'

Soon, the astonished Afghan soldiers saw, open-mouthed, the Naga warriors towing two soldiers each, as if dragging dead pigs, holding some by their hair, others by their legs and hands. The dragging sounds were horrifying. The metal armours of the Afghani soldiers scraped the ground, leaving trails in the dust. The cries of the injured lingered in the chilly evening air. The sight was one of utter despair. Narayan, strong and frightening, looked into the eyes of a wounded soldier he was dragging. There was no pity in his eyes, only the fire of battle and a hint of viciousness. 'Fear not,' he mocked with a sinister smile, 'you'll be with your dead brothers soon.'

Across the field, another Naga laughed maniacally, yanking the chain tied to a group of injured soldiers. 'Come, come! Let's feast!' he shouted mockingly.

'Hurry up and drag them faster. I can't bear the hunger anymore,' shouted another Naga.

The remaining Afghan soldiers, those few who had managed to escape the onslaught, stood back in horror. The sight of their fellow soldiers being taken, and the ominous laughter of the Nagas, was spine-chilling. Right before disappearing into the shadows, the Nagas turned towards the terrified Afghan soldiers, staring into their eyes with eerie smiles. Standing and looking at their fellow soldiers being dragged to death, the Afghans knew what fate awaited their mates. To them, the Nagas did not look tired . . . they looked hungry and excited. It was more than enough for all the Afghan soldiers to imagine that the same could be their fate on the next day of fighting, if they were left injured yet alive.

As the Nagas disappeared into the darkness, the grim scene remained imprinted in the Afghan soldiers' minds, a reminder of the ferocity and ruthlessness of the Naga sadhus.

'These madmen could have simply killed them all; why put so much effort into taking them alive?' one Afghan soldier cried.

'I have heard that they feed on the raw flesh of living humans,' another replied in fear.

'That is why they don't die,' said a third.

'Promise me that you will kill me if you see me injured and helpless, and I shall do the same for you,' said one of the Afghans to his fellows. The rest looked at each other for the same kind of assurance.

*

A stream of Nagas flooded into the treatment camp. Though minorly injured with bleeding wounds, they arrived with gracious smiles. The victory of the day was evident on their faces. The sadhvis rushed around dressing their wounds. As Dhruv lay there watching the brave Nagas, Ajaa walked into the hut. After examining all the sadhus, he came up to Dhruv and inspected his wounds.

'You have almost recovered, Dhruv. Soon, you will be ready to walk,' said Ajaa.

His confidence filled Dhruv with hope that he would soon fight alongside him. He thanked Ajaa and then fell back on his bed.

After attending to Dhruv and the injured Naga sadhus from the first day of the intense battle, Ajaa found himself standing at the edge of the same cliff, looking in the direction of the narrow passage. It was the same route that Shambhu ji, Vanraaj and the others had taken to escort the people to safety. His gaze was fixed on that distant path and the burden of the battle's aftermath weighed heavily on his shoulders.

From a distance, Adhiraj was observing Ajaa again, like the previous night, but this time, he chose not to intrude, instead making his way to the Mathadhish, who sat in meditation. With a respectful bow, Adhiraj joined the Mathadhish on the ground, finding solace in the sage's presence.

As the two sat in contemplative silence, Adhiraj finally spoke. 'Ajaa's unwavering determination on the battlefield was admirable, but there is something different about him when he is alone. He is in pain as he does not have answers to the questions about his past.' The Mathadhish opened his eyes and met Adhiraj's gaze. 'Would you like to hear a story, Adhiraj?' asked the Mathadhish. Adhiraj nodded, eager to hear and perhaps find some insight into the complexities of Ajaa's inner world.

Nearly thirty-five years ago, there was a vast kingdom in the extreme north of God-land, ruled by a young king named Dhyanendra. A mysterious Naga sadhu entered the kingdom. He was a wanderer, clothed in tattered rags, his long dreadlocks trailing behind him. He appeared to be in his forties, and while crossing this kingdom, found hundreds of dead bodies with nobody to cremate them and many hundreds of men, women and children suffering from some kind of strange sickness. The people of the kingdom believed it was someone's curse but the Naga sadhu knew that a deadly epidemic was spreading in the kingdom like wildfire. People were succumbing one after another, and no cure could be found. The people were desperately trying to save themselves, but to no avail. The cremation grounds were constantly being prepared.

The Naga asked the people of the kingdom about the king. He learnt that King Dhyanendra was a beloved and highly respected king and was always concerned about his kingdom's future. The Naga understood that the king was being tested and that the gods were teaching him that kings could be helpless too. However, the king had remained resolute in his duty to protect his people.

The Naga sadhu reached the gates of the king's fort and demanded a meeting with King Dhyanendra. The guards refused and said that the king's beloved wife was expecting a child, so he could not expose them to this catastrophic situation.

'Tell your king that I am going to break this curse for his people and save his kingdom from extinction. I need nine men who will make sure that there will be a constant supply of the materials needed for the cure during my yajna,' said the Naga.

The message was relayed to the king, and, in no time, the Naga sadhu was granted all that he had demanded. Amid the despair of the epidemic, he sat in the heart of the kingdom and initiated a yagna, dancing in a trance as he swayed to an ethereal rhythm, his own *damru* in his hand. The rhythmic beats of the damru echoed through the kingdom, drawing people's attention.

The Naga's dance around the yagna was a mesmerizing spectacle. His body twisted and turned with an otherworldly grace and his dreadlocks swirled around him. His eyes remained closed as he chanted ancient Sanskrit incantations, invoking the divine forces. The flames of the yagna leapt higher, burning brightly with a vibrant, almost supernatural glow. With each rhythmic beat of his damru, it seemed as though the very fabric of reality was being rewoven. Amid his dance, he regularly took some herbs from the soldiers and continued throwing them into the fire. The next morning, he asked the people to dissolve the remains in the local well and serve it to the sick.

The people believed that the Naga had used some kind of otherworldly magic. The epidemic began to subside, and people stopped dying. King Dhyanendra's trusted men saw the spectacle with their own eyes. They visited the king and mentioned that the Naga was using his mantras, divine herbs and remedies to heal the people of the kingdom.

As word of the Naga's miraculous presence and his healing yagna spread, the king couldn't ignore the profound impact he had on his suffering subjects. One by one, their pain was relieved, and hope began to walk again on the once-empty streets.

After the Naga had miraculously erased the disease and brought a glimmer of hope to the kingdom, King Dhyanendra ventured to meet him personally, overwhelmed with gratitude and joy, his curiosity piqued by the enigmatic sage's extraordinary abilities. He expressed his deep indebtedness and said, 'O sage! Demand what you desire in exchange for saving the lives of my people and consider it gifted to you before you even ask for it.'

The Naga remained an unreadable and unexpressive figure, his enigmatic silence adding to the air of mystique that surrounded him. He looked at the king and said, 'I need nothing.'

This was unusual for the king, so he insisted, 'I am the king and kings must not be indebted. It will be a lifelong burden on me that I cannot bear to live with, and I can't die before repaying this debt either. I live for my people, and I can die to protect them, so I promise you, whatever you ask for is yours, even if it's my kingdom or my life. Just ask for it and free me of this debt, dear sage.'

The sadhu took a few seconds before he spoke. 'At this moment I don't need anything, mighty king, but when I need something, I will return to you. When that time comes, remember the promise you have just made. I will make a demand and you will have to honour it.'

'You have my word, sage,' said King Dhyanendra.

The sage continued on his way north and the kingdom rose to prosperity again, stronger and full of renewed hope.

A few years passed and King Dhyanendra became the father of a healthy child, a son. The king's joy knew no bounds. It was now time for a celebration in his kingdom. He celebrated and initiated charitable acts to spread happiness throughout the kingdom, and the people rejoiced.

Amid the celebration, the same Naga returned and demanded to meet King Dhyanendra. He was presented in front of the king. The king stood up from his throne and greeted the Naga with a warm hug. He washed the sadhu's feet with his own hands, made him sit on his throne, sat at his feet and asked, 'You chose such an auspicious day to return, dear sage. I am very happy as my kingdom has got their next generation king, my firstborn boy. What brings you to me, dear sage?'

'Your promise,' replied the Naga, with a poker-face, looking into the king's eyes.

'A warrior never forgets his promise, and I too remember mine. Ask whatever you want, and it will be yours,' said the king, smiling, with his hands folded in front of the sage.

The sage remained silent for quite some time as he knew that what he was going to demand was going to silence the whole kingdom. The king continued looking at the sage with a smile, waiting for him to make his demand, and then the sage spoke, 'I demand that your newborn child and you leave this kingdom forever and come with me.'

The smile vanished from the king's face. There was complete silence in the courtyard. The Naga cryptically uttered, 'You said you could give me your life and your kingdom too. Now honour your promise.' The Naga's demand put everything at a momentary pause, leaving the kingdom in suspense as the people tried to fathom the reason behind this mysterious demand.

The king ordered each and every one of his trusted men to leave the courtyard. In a minute, there were just two men in the courtyard, one who looked like a beggar but was sitting on the throne, and another who looked like the king but was sitting on the floor.

'I am bound to keep my promise and I will, but I wish to know why you are asking this of me,' asked the king humbly.

The Naga replied, 'The Nagas are the protectors of dharma. They are rigorously trained and disciplined, but none of them are from the bloodline of rulers and kings. They are a great army without a commander. I demand you lead them and expand the army against the enemies of dharma.'

'And why my son?' asked the king helplessly.

'You are brave yet humble, strong yet sacrificing, a warrior that worships. You have servants, yet you wish to serve people. No one but your son can succeed you and no one but you can prepare your son for the next generation of Naga warriors.'

Being a man of his word, King Dhyanendra made the heart-wrenching decision of leaving his kingdom along with his infant to fulfil his vow to the Naga. He called upon his two most trusted commanders, entrusting them with the protection of the kingdom and the royal family until their last breath.

The next morning, the queen and all his trusted men saw the ritual that converted a warrior king to a Naga warrior forever.

'Rituals! What rituals?' asked Thomas.

The Naga explained: Every Naga sadhu had to undergo a series of rituals to break all shackles and cycles of lives and deaths. All his ties with his karmic connections were broken, his relations with the dead or alive, his memories of the past, his present and dreams of the future. The king's costume and crown were removed, all his jewellery was placed in a large bowl and his head was shaved. He was made to perform the last rites of each and every family member, dead or alive. Tears rolled down his eyes when he performed the last rites of his two-month-old son, who was alive and crying in the arms of the Naga, and his beloved queen, who herself was crying at her own death ritual, which was being performed by her own husband. At last, the king was ordered to conduct his own last rites to establish his death in the material world and ensure that no connections with his mortal life remained.

It was now time for King Dhyanendra to leave his kingdom in the dark with his infant, who was still crying in the heartless Naga's arms. As the three were about to leave, the queen kissed her son's forehead, cried and said to the king, 'At least my son will have his father with him all his life.'

'And I will protect him with my life,' King Dhyanendra promised the queen.

The Naga standing beside them spoke again, calling the king by his name, and this time, what he asked for was even more heart-rending than his last demand. The Naga said, 'Dhyanendra! You have no relationship with this infant anymore. He is an orphan now. He is not your son. He belongs to the Nagas now and under no condition will you ever reveal your true name and identity to him or to anybody in the society of Nagas. Your allegiance lies with me, and you will join us as a Naga with no attachments.'

'As you command!' said Dhyanendra, who had just realized that he was no longer a king, a husband or a father—he was just a Naga warrior, serving the gods and protecting dharma.

As the Mathadhish concluded the story, Adhiraj looked contemplative. He finally asked, 'But how is this thirty-five-year-old tale relevant to our time now?'

The Mathadhish revealed, 'Adhiraj, the king, Dhyanendra, was given a new name after reaching the Naga camp. He is now famous as Shambhu ji.'

'Why did you tell me this?' asked Adhiraj suspiciously.

'Because you wanted the answers to the questions about Ajaa's past. Ajaa was the newborn, the prince,' replied the Mathadhish.

'And how do you know all this?' asked Adhiraj.

'I am nearly seventy-five years old now. What was the age of the Naga who visited the kingdom of King Dhyanendra thirty-five years ago? Do the maths.'

'Why did you tell this tale today, after thirty-five years?' asked Adhiraj, realizing that the Naga who had made the demand was none other than the Mathadhish himself.

'Because tomorrow may be our last day alive, and Ajaa's truth was a burden on me too, just a little less heavier than on Shambhu. Now I have to go and show myself to the Afghan soldiers before they die,' said the Mathadhish, getting up and leaving Adhiraj perplexed.

'But still! Why did you trust me with this story?' Adhiraj asked again.

The Mathadhish stopped, looked at Adhiraj and said, 'Because I know who you are.'

Adhiraj was stunned by the Mathadhish's look and revelation, wondering how the Mathadhish knew about his true identity, but decided not to question the old sadhu any further. Adhiraj kept mum and the Mathadhish kept walking. The Mathadhish suddenly turned towards Adhiraj and said, 'Thank you, Adhiraj, or whatever your name is, for being a part of this battle. Keep our dharma alive after our deaths too.'

Adhiraj bowed to the wise old man before he turned back and walked to the Afghan soldiers.

Sardar's tent was dimly lit by a solitary lamp, its flickering flame casting an ominous glow. He sat there, deep in thought, his eyes revealing the weight of the day's losses. The haunting cries of the captured Afghan soldiers and the triumphant roars of the Nagas echoed in his ears. The tent was filled with the hushed murmurings of his commanders. The atmosphere was tense and dismal, reflecting the sombre mood of the soldiers outside. The devastating loss, compounded by the distressing sight of their fellow soldiers being dragged away, had left a mark.

'The morale of our troops is fragile. Many men are talking of the dark legends surrounding the Naga sadhus, huzoor,' said one of the commanders, his voice filled with concern. 'They whisper in fear that the Nagas are cannibals, feasting on the flesh and organs of their enemies and drinking their blood to gain inhuman powers. Our soldiers are horror-struck by the way the Nagas dragged away those men, by the terrifying delight in their monstrous eyes.'

Turning to his trusted commander, Sardar inquired, 'Zafar, when are the cannons arriving?'

'They will be in position before the first light tomorrow. The terrain is treacherous and is slowing their progress,' replied Zafar.

Sardar smirked, his eyes glinting with menace. 'Great. Tomorrow, with the cannons, we will strike with renewed force. We will remind our soldiers and the Nagas why we are to be feared. It will be a sight to behold—the sky darkened with cannon smoke and the ground shaking with their thunder. Tomorrow, I will bury them alive and stand atop the cliff of their dead bodies. Tomorrow, Gokul will bow before me,' said Sardar Khan.

With the imagination of chaos and destruction, Sardar Khan's eyes were shining bright for the next morning but as the darkness settled, whispers spread like wildfire through the camp and the tales of the Naga sadhus grew ever more elaborate, instilling a mix of awe and fear among the soldiers.

Not far from Gokul, Vedant and his army were approaching from the north. His commander-in-chief, Krishna, was leading the brigade of 2500 soldiers, 100 elephants, 100 horses and ten moveable cannons. Jugal Kishore with his forces was also on the move.

15

Prisoners of War

The next morning, something unexpected happened in Sardar's camp. The dawn was about to break. Sardar Khan and his commanders were eagerly awaiting the arrival of the cannons when a young soldier, out of breath and dust-covered, burst into the tent. He stood there for a few seconds, panting, before the commander asked him to speak.

'All the soldiers taken by the Naga sadhus . . . they have returned!' exclaimed the young soldier.

A stunned silence filled the tent.

'Where are they? asked Zafar.

The young soldier pointed, then led the way. A crowd had gathered around the returned soldiers. They seemed shaken but unharmed. Their wounds were covered with white and saffron bandages.

Zafar approached the group. 'Speak! What did they do to you?'

One of the returned soldiers, eyes wide with a mix of fear and relief, replied, 'They did nothing. They treated our wounds, served us food, gave us water and released us in the morning.'

The revelation left many in the camp bewildered. This unexpected act of mercy contrasted vastly with the rumours they had heard. The morale of Sardar's army, already fragile, now teetered on an edge.

Just then, Sardar joined them with the first light of the sun, his tall frame casting a shadow.

'The cannons have arrived,' informed Zafar.

Sardar looked up, his face a blend of relief and newfound determination. He responded, his voice steady, 'Perfect. Deploy them immediately. Today is the end of this madness.'

Zafar nodded, understanding the gravity of the situation. 'We will be ready to fire in an hour.'

Sardar leaned forward, his eyes sharp. 'The Nagas won't anticipate the devastation our cannons will bring to them.'

Zafar agreed, 'The element of surprise will be on our side. The Nagas won't expect such firepower.'

Sardar clenched his fist, his resolve hardening. 'Prepare the men.'

The long barrels of the cannons shone brightly that morning. Twenty cannons were lined up in formation, aimed at the Naga base and the centre of Gokul. Each cannon was guarded by several soldiers, many of whom were already wounded from the day before. The cannon was moved in place after positioning the artillery. Each shell was a hollow iron ball filled with gunpowder.

Ajaa stood amid the Naga warriors, wounds from yesterday's battle still fresh, surrounded by the remaining Naga sadhus. Although their spirit remained undeterred, they weren't prepared for what lay ahead. The first day of battle, which had been a success for the Nagas, with no casualties, had infuriated Sardar Khan and he wanted to kill each and every Naga and destroy Gokul completely.

The once serene horizon of Gokul, dotted with humble huts and sacred temples, was about to face the wrath of Sardar Khan's artillery.

In the Afghan camp, adrenaline ran high as everyone awaited Sardar Khan's orders. Among them were the soldiers who had been sent back from the Naga camp. Scattered unevenly in different formations, the returned soldiers were also apprehensive, their hearts beating fast. As they waited, the men cleaned the barrels of the cannons with damp sponges to remove any residue.

'Load the shot,' shouted Sardar Khan's artillery commander. The cannonballs were filled with gunpowder and loaded into the barrels.

'Take aim.' The soldiers took aim as a small amount of fine gunpowder was placed at the vent that the gunner would ignite.

'Ready to fire.' Everyone held their breaths. It seemed as if time had stopped. There was an eerie silence.

'FIRE!' The gunners set the priming powder alight which, in turn, ignited the main charge, propelling shots out of the cannons. The sound of twenty shots being fired at once was deafening. Smoke erupted in all directions like hundreds of volcanoes exploding one after another. Sardar Khan's eyes remained fixed on the horizon as Gokul came burning down.

The thunderous explosion sent shockwaves through the village. The once sturdy walls of houses crumbled like dry bread under the pressure. The temples, symbols of hope and devotion, weren't spared either. Their walls bore the brunt of the charge, with sacred idols being blown apart. Naga sadhus stood, watching in shock, helpless and outraged as the temple bells, which once rang to summon the devotees for prayers, now clanged wildly from the impact.

'Take cover! Spread out as widely as you can!' yelled Ajaa. If the Nagas were to scatter in different directions, it might keep them safe, otherwise one well-placed shot from Sardar's cannons would kill them all.

One such cannon unfortunately hit a boulder behind which five Naga sadhus were taking cover. The boulder blew apart, killing the Nagas instantly. Ajaa and the Mathadhish helplessly watched the death of their five brothers. These were the first lives that were lost from the Naga's side but unfortunately not the last.

As the sun climbed higher, dark plumes of smoke replaced the natural serenity. The Naga sadhus were smeared with their own blood. The very ground they considered sacred was being desecrated before their eyes.

The Yamuna flowing through Gokul, once clear and reflective of the blue skies, was now muddied with dirt and blood. The green fields, which were on the brink of yielding a harvest, were now scorched, leaving behind a barren wasteland. The haunting cries of the injured echoed in the smoke and chaos. Sacred scriptures were burnt to ash and the once harmonious rhythm of Gokul was disrupted, perhaps forever.

The treatment camps were not spared either. Many huts and tents had caught fire. A few huts were directly hit, destroying them and killing a sadhvi inside.

Once the shelling had stopped, Ajaa assembled the Naga warriors. Their main focus had shifted from mounting an offensive to saving as many lives as possible. No number of bandages seemed enough for the wounded. The Nagas who had fallen victim to the day's attack grimaced in pain, but tried to hold their own so their fellow Nagas could defend their land, even if it was at the cost of their lives. And as the dust began to settle, the scale of the devastation became apparent. Gokul, a symbol of spirituality and peace, now bore the scars of a merciless assault. The Nagas were bleeding.

Meanwhile, King Vedant was still half a day away.

Reviewing the situation, Ajaa rushed to the Mathadhish. 'It's time for our next move! Order them to run.'

'You are right, Ajaa. It's time,' agreed the Mathadhish, his eyes fierce and determined.

The Nagas' three fastest runners from Cheetah Dasta, identified through the friendly race conducted by the Mathadhish before the war started, Namah, Bhola and Shivay, were summoned by the Mathadhish and they stood in front of him, awaiting their orders.

'Go. Fulfil the promise you made to Lord Shiva,' said the Mathadhish.

The young Nagas touched the Mathadhish's feet in respect, bidding a final goodbye.

Then the young Nagas lined up on their marks and held their crouching positions, their heads low. The Mathadhish said in a fierce tone, as if starting a racing competition, 'Namah . . . Bhola . . . Shivay . . . run!' And the young Nagas sprinted, screaming, towards Sardar's humongous army.

Sardar Khan's army couldn't believe their eyes as they saw the three young Nagas run at lightning speed towards them. They had no weapons in their hands and no war cry came out of their mouths as they ran like cheetahs, racing each other, searching for something in the huge crowd of Afghan soldiers. They were seemingly on a suicide mission. From the opposite end, Sardar Khan, bewildered by the audacity of the three, muttered, 'Madness at its peak . . . naked idiots!' Their sprint towards death was beyond anybody's understanding. Sardar Khan yelled an order, 'Archers! Ready!'

As arrows soared through the air, the sprinters looked at each other and it seemed as if they all changed gears, suddenly running at twice their earlier speed. While the arrows descended one by one, the charging Nagas kept going, their determination unwavering. Arrows stuck out of their bodies, reducing their speed but failing to stop them. It was as if they were seeking something in the enemy hordes.

'What are they up to? What are they searching for?' Sardar Khan murmured to himself, looking at their speed, determination and the quest in their eyes.

As they ran, each Naga sadhu felt the weight of their dead brothers who had been crushed and killed in the cannon bombarding minutes ago.

Namah, one of the three young Naga sadhus, finally found what he was looking for and shouted to his mates, 'I found one.' Bhola and Shivay, the other two young Nagas, replied one after another, 'I have spotted a few targets too.' As they screamed to each other, it was loud enough for Sardar Khan to hear them loud and clear, as by then they were quite close to the enemy's army. Sardar Khan and his commanders were still wondering what was motivating these three young Nagas to certain death. Their targets were the wounded soldiers sent back to Sardar Khan that same morning. They could easily be identified as each injured soldier's wounds had been dressed in a peculiar saffron and white colour that set them apart from their counterparts in green and black. Pierced with arrows and panting with fatigue after their sprint, the Naga sadhus looked at each other and smiled.

'Har Har Mahadev!' they screamed in unison, looking at the wounded soldiers sent back alive. As the cry of 'Har Har Mahadev' reached the ears of the soldiers who had been captured by the Nagas the day before and returned alive, they suddenly turned on their own comrades. All hell broke loose in the ranks of Sardar's army.

One of the soldiers, eyes wide and crazed, sprinted towards a pile of explosives, setting himself on fire. The explosion rocked the ground, taking out a significant portion of Sardar's forces. Another soldier, in a frenzy, lodged himself inside a cannon's mouth and lit its fuse. The cannon exploded, blowing him and a few soldiers to smithereens. The remaining wounded soldiers wrapped in saffron started attacking and killing their own army like zombies unleashed.

Sardar, in utter disbelief, cried, 'Hold your positions! Fight back!' But the damage was already done. Before they could recover, the Naga archers unleashed a volley of arrows, bringing more soldiers down. In no time, Sardar Khan's army was under attack both from inside and outside, breaking all its formations and shattering all strategies. The army was ready for everything from the Naga warriors . . . but not this. They didn't know where to focus as they were now being attacked by their own soldiers as well as the adversary.

As Sardar Khan watched his army run around in a frenzy, one of the Naga sadhus reached up to his carriage and stood right in front of him. The last dying Naga runner looked at Sardar and laughed.

'Why did the Afghans start attacking on their own after hearing Har Har Mahadev?' asked the hiker in the cave.

The nameless Naga answered, 'It was all planned in advance on the previous night by Ajaa. The night before, it had been the Mathadhish who had ordered the Naga warriors to gather the wounded Afghan soldiers. That's why, after the conversation with Adhiraj about Ajaa's past, the Mathadhish said that the Afghan soldiers had to see him before they die. They then handpicked thirty soldiers who would be capable of fighting again after treatment at their camp. After their wounds had been dressed, the thirty soldiers were led to his hut where, with his mystical powers, the Mathadhish hypnotized them, programming them to attack when they heard "Har Har Mahadev".'

As Sardar and his men retreated, the Nagas stood straight in triumph, their spirits lifted but their hearts bleeding tears for the loss of those who had died that day, including the sadhvi and the three young sadhus, Namah, Bhola and Shivay, who gave their lives to run and wake the hypnotized. But against all odds, the Nagas had held their ground for another day. The cannons were almost destroyed; those left had no cannonballs.

Gokul was a different place now. Once a vibrant village, full of laughter and life, it was now a mosaic of pain, ashes and smouldering fires. The aftermath of Sardar Khan's assault was a scene of sheer devastation.

Ruins of homes and temples stood silent witnesses to the horror unleashed on Gokul. Smoky tendrils curled up towards the evening sky, carrying with them the smell of burning wood and sorrow. The cannon fire had given way to an eerie silence.

In the middle of this wreckage, the remaining sadhvis showcased their strength and resilience. Dressed in white, they became beacons of hope, working tirelessly to help the injured Nagas, their hands covered in blood and medicinal herbs. The anguish in their eyes was evident, but their determination to help the wounded was even stronger.

A makeshift camp had been erected and the injured Nagas lay on mats, their wounds being attended to by the sadhvis. The tent was filled with the scent of medicinal herbs, and only the occasional groan of pain broke the grieving silence.

Not too far away, under the shade of a large banyan tree, Ajaa and the Mathadhish were deep in conversation, their faces lined with concern.

'We have lost too many,' said the Mathadhish, his voice heavy with grief.

Ajaa nodded. 'But they haven't died in vain. Darkness is upon us now, and it's time to burn the bodies of our martyrs. Their ashes will be our cloak tomorrow.'

'Ajaa, the remaining Nagas will look to you for strength and guidance. We need a plan, a way to surprise Sardar Khan and throw him off balance,' mused the Mathadhish.

'I have hope that help will arrive in time,' replied Ajaa.

In the opposite camp, as the sun began to dip below the horizon, casting shades of saffron over the land, Sardar Khan stood tall amid his commanders, the formidable backdrop of his entire army behind him. His face was a mask of anger and determination.

Maps of the region were spread out, riddled with marks and notes. The continuous clamour of the military camp outside was a grim reminder of the devastation they had endured.

Sardar's trusted commander walked in, his face strained from the fighting of the last two days. But he stood erect as he gave Sardar his report: 'I have the counts you ordered.'

Sardar Khan looked up, nodding for him to proceed.

Zafar took a deep breath. 'Out of our original 4000 men, only 2300 remain combat ready. Our cavalry of horses and camels is safe and ready to enter the battleground. We have lost a significant number of cannons. Thankfully, some can be repaired and will be ready in a few hours.'

Sardar Khan leaned back, absorbing the news. 'Such losses in just two days . . .' he muttered, his gaze focused on the map. 'I'll admit, I underestimated these unclothed nomads. I never expected these naked, unruly babas to be so gifted in battle. Their tactics, their knowledge of warfare . . . it has all caught me off guard.'

He addressed the commander of the horse and camel regiment. 'You! Tomorrow, you will lead the charge. I expected the end of these Nagas in the first hour. Yet, here we are, on day two, still facing resistance. This ends tomorrow. Crush them with your speed and strength.'

The commander nodded. 'My lord, they will be wiped off the face of the earth.'

Meanwhile, that night, King Vedant had reached one of the cliffs on the outskirts of Gokul, high enough to review the situation. He now stood at a place where the battle ground was clearly visible to him. Jugal Kishore and his troops were still marching towards Gokul. Though they were moving without halts, they were still a day's journey away.

In Gokul, Ajaa and his fellow Naga sadhus conducted the Bhasmaarti and the final rites for their fallen brothers. More than a quarter of Ajaa's sadhus had been killed in a single day. As the burning bodies became ash and the light seeped away into darkness, the Nagas gathered their resolve. They applied the *bhasma* (ashes) of their own brothers on their bodies and chanted mantras and prayers. With every passing second, their determination to save their dharma grew robust and more concrete.

16

The Final Battle

The sky had never seemed as dark as it did that night. No body knew if they were awake to stop the night from passing or waiting for the morning that would bring more blood. The first light of dawn painted the sky in hues of orange and pink, but to the men watching, it looked red. Dhruv stood at the boundary of Gokul, contemplating the ruins.

The village, which had become a battleground, was tiredly preparing to face another wave of death. The Nagas were ready for the next day, their bodies smeared in the ashes of their own brothers. Dhruv saw Ajaa emerge from the ruins, his face stern, yet with a certain softness in his eyes. 'Dhruv,' he began, his voice deep and resonant, 'You have recovered enough to undertake your next journey. Time will heal the rest of you. It's time for you to leave.'

Dhruv looked at him, feeling a mix of confusion and anxiety. 'I won't leave. I am not a coward. I want to die with all of you on the battlefield. We are at the turning point of a great battle,' said Dhruv, pleading.

Ajaa took a deep breath and replied, 'Death doesn't win battles and wars. Wars are won by the living. This battle is just the beginning—a beginning so small that it may not get even a line when history is penned. Wearing death here is easy, but I see you are meant for a bigger burden—the burden of life. As the commander of this battalion of the protectors of dharma, I order you to stay alive and walk towards the Himalayas to enlighten others about what has happened here. The Nagas in the Himalayas possess powers and knowledge that can stop the waves of invaders coming our way in the future. They are our only hope to turn the tide against this immoral filth.'

Dhruv pondered Ajaa's words, his fingers running through the prayer beads around his neck. 'So you want me to go and seek their help?'

Ajaa nodded. 'Yes, you are the bridge between the Nagas dying here and the Nagas in the Himalayas. It is your destiny to register, document and report what has happened here. That will unite us all and bring about an alliance with the numbers, strength and power to defeat Ahmad Shah Abdali and his army. The war has just begun and will last for centuries. Our enemies will increase and invade like the plague. We shall be the antidote. Many civilizations will perish and many will convert. What will survive in the times to come are the Trinity, trident and temples. If you want to be a true soldier, then learn to take orders and finish the task given, at any cost. Let that cost be not your life, but the life of the one who stops you. Your journey to Gokul, despite your injuries, taught me the level of your dedication towards your goals. You speak well, you were a teacher and you can write. You are young and strong, and you can travel. I am not suspending you from your duties. I am just giving you a purpose bigger than this battle, your life and your death. Now go, my friend! The Nagas in the Himalayas await your arrival.'

The weight of the responsibility dawned on Dhruv. He looked at Ajaa with determination. 'I will not let you down. I will tell all of this to the world. I will bring all the Nagas from the white mountains to the red lands.'

Ajaa placed a hand on Dhruv's shoulder. 'Remember, if you fail, many generations will die before they can even be born. Our gods will be counted as myths and will perish with other civilizations as if they never existed. Your survival now decides the survival or extinction of your dharma. Now get going. Every moment counts. May Shiva be with you, Dhruv. Find our comrades, tell them what transpired in Gokul and what is still to come.'

Dhruv gave a final nod, determination burning in his eyes, and set out for the towering peaks of the Himalayas, carrying with him the hopes and fates of the Nagas of Gokul.

Meanwhile, Sardar Khan's tent was dimly lit by the rays of the rising sun. He walked out, taking in the 2300 men, 100 camels and 200 horses waiting for their orders. Then he addressed his army. 'Sons of Allah! I had thought we would triumph in mere hours. But the Nagas, despite their losses, still stand. Today, we will go all out. We will show no mercy. We will end this, once and for all!' The army roared in response, their spirits reignited by their leader's commitment.

The commander-in-chief nodded slowly, sharing his leader's sentiments. 'Their spirituality does not make them weak, like we thought. Instead, it fuels their resolve.'

Sardar Khan smirked. 'But that ends today. Employ every man we have. I want the camels to be stationed in the last line, right with the remaining cannons. I want them alive to load our carts—every necklace will go with the neck it belongs to, every earring with its ear, every anklet with its foot and every bangle with its hand.'

'Yes, my lord,' the commander-in-chief acknowledged.

Sardar Khan paused for a moment and his gaze hardened. 'Today is the final day of the battle for Gokul. I won't rest, not until I see the grandeur of Gokul reduced to rubble, and the very grounds stained with the blood of those Naga sadhus.'

His commander-in-chief saluted again. 'As you wish, Sardar. Gokul will be yours.'

Meanwhile, after bidding farewell to Dhruv, Ajaa and the Mathadhish sat facing each other. Ajaa sighed, his face leaden with concern. 'Mathadhish, after the last two days, only sixty-three of our Naga brothers remain fit for battle.'

The Mathadhish closed his eyes briefly, absorbing the news. 'In our hearts roar the spirit of thousands. Every Naga, with his faith and strength, is a force to reckon with.'

Ajaa nodded, his determination hardening. 'Although the odds we face today are overwhelming, I believe in our cause, and in the stubborn spirit of our brothers.'

The Mathadhish looked deep into Ajaa's eyes, his voice firm: 'Remember, Ajaa. Our duty is to defend our land, our faith. Each of us has a destiny to fulfil.'

Inspired, Ajaa stood up with renewed vigour. 'Then let's prepare for our destiny. We will rally our remaining brothers and prepare for the future.'

Both leaders made their way to their fellow Nagas.

Ajaa stepped into the centre, the mantle of leadership settling on his shoulders. Adhiraj blew the shankh, all the remaining sixty-three Naga sadhus gathered, their faces showing the signs of battle but the fire in their eyes undimmed.

Ajaa took a moment, a deep breath to ground himself, then addressed the group, 'The ashes on your body are a sign that our fallen brothers are still with us and fighting for their dharma. We now wear them on our skin. Remember their sacrifices and fight for them. It is time we end the war and take revenge for our brothers and for dharma. Consider the rudraksh beads encircling our necks,' Ajaa continued, fingers grazing the beads on his own neck. 'They are not mere adornments, but emblems of focus, symbols of our devotion. With each bead, we are reminded of the prayers we have chanted, the meditations we have dived into, the depths of our minds we've explored.

'And our bare bodies,' he proclaimed, his voice rising, 'our most poignant statement. Stripped of armour, we stand vulnerable yet strong, raw yet refined, exposed yet enigmatic. We need no armour, for our spirit is our shield. Our nakedness is our audacity, our proclamation that we fear nothing, for we have nothing to lose.

'Today, brothers, we stand on the cliff of a defining moment. Our land, our dharma, calls out for each one of us. And as we have always done, we will answer. We have been sculpted by the harshest of environments, by the toughest of challenges. We are not just warriors; we are the embodiment of Shiva's rage.

'As we march forward, know this: we do not go into this battle hoping for victory. We go knowing victory is ours. Let the world gaze upon us and know that we, the Naga warriors, aren't just monks; we are the guardians of this land's spirit, its very soul.

'Let's march ahead, brothers. With every step, we will shake the earth, with every chant, we will drown out the cries of our enemies, and with every swing of our weapons, we will carve our destiny with their deaths.'

The air was thick with palpable energy; the very ground seemed to thrum in unison with Ajaa's words, readying them for the battle that lay ahead.

In the crowd, emotions swirled—from doubt to determination, from fear to fierce resolve. But one sentiment emerged above them all—unity. The Naga sadhus, each with his own thoughts and feelings, were united under the banner of their purpose, their legacy and the challenge that lay ahead.

He continued, 'Brothers, the dawn has brought forth the greatest challenge we've ever faced. The enemy thinks that our brothers are dead, and we have been reduced in numbers. They don't know what we are but promise me that they will not die in the bliss of ignorance. Promise me that their souls will abandon their bodies in fear of the death that will resemble our faces. Their spirits must leave our lands, betraying their bodies, which we will later bury so that they can be used as manure for the next crop season. I command you all to invoke the spirits of our dead brothers in you. We stepped in this land together for a purpose. We will leave this world together after accomplishing it. Till then, the souls of our brothers will be in us and will wait to leave with us. Let us borrow their strength and illuminate the path for the future generations to come. To the souls that I can see and to the souls that I cannot, I urge and I command, let the dead and the living fight shoulder to shoulder against the enemies of dharma.'

One of the Nagas shouted, 'For dharma!' and the echo 'For dharma!' resounded, their voices merging in a unified war chorus, ready for the final battle.

As the two armies assembled, the early morning mist that had settled over the battlefield was pierced by the golden rays of the sun. On one side stood Sardar Khan's massive army, seemingly invincible in their numbers. Against them were sixty-three resolute and fearless Naga sadhus.

From another vantage point, on a distant hilltop, King Vedant and his commander-in-chief, Krishna, atop their horses, observed the imminent battle. Vedant's 2500 men stood in formation behind them, their armour shimmering in the morning light.

It was a dismal view. They quietly observed the ruins, the temples burnt in the aftermath of the shelling. An earnest man, Krishna was in tears at the sight.

'Maharaj, at no cost can we let Sardar Khan win. We must seek revenge against the Afghans. These temples that held our roots, the memories of our ancestors for centuries, have been destroyed within seconds. How can anyone be so heartless? What is the point of all this?'

King Vedant assessed the situation and then spoke. 'What is that place?' He pointed at some open land not far from Gokul.

'That must be the Naga base. They seem to have taken quite a few hits themselves! We must go and help them now!' urged Krishna.

'Wait, Krishna. I see some movement there. I don't think it's over yet. Sardar won't stop until his men raid the town completely. We must assess the situation before getting into it. We will wait for some time, but keep the men ready,' said Vedant.

'As you say, my lord,' said Krishna, deferring to his young king. Vedant continued to watch; meanwhile, Jugal Kishore was about to reach Gokul from the other direction.

17

Nandi Descends

The stage was set for the showdown between Ajaa and Sardar Khan. The golden sun had barely kissed the horizon when the cacophony of war erupted on the fields of Gokul.

The earth trembled beneath the weight of clattering hooves as the 200 horsemen from Sardar Khan's army charged forward, their spears gleaming and eyes filled with bloodlust.

Leading the vanguard of the Naga sadhus was Ajaa, his face painted with the sacred ash of his dead brothers. His eyes darted in every direction, scanning for the slightest gap or break in the enemy's formation. Beside him, the Mathadhish, Adhiraj and Narayan used their superior agility to create whirlwinds of death, darting between horses, parrying blows and retaliating with deadly precision. Their mastery in combat made it clear why they were the revered leaders of the Naga order.

The clang of metal meeting metal resonated through the battlefield as weapons clashed with one another. It was almost rhythmic, like the beating heart of the battle itself. In between were intermittent thuds and crashes, the sounds of bodies falling—of warriors and horses alike. The air was thick with the stench of blood, sweat and gunpowder.

The Nagas were falling one after the other but were taking tens of Afghan soldiers with them. One of the Nagas, whose spear moved like an extension of his own arm, found himself surrounded. He fought valiantly, parrying and thrusting, his war cry echoing across the battlefield, until he was taken down, a spear lodged into his back. Another Naga, his khadga swinging like a crescent moon, cut down several adversaries before being overwhelmed by sheer numbers. Two more Nagas, one with an axe and another with a sword, met similar fates.

The sadhvis treating the wounded knew that those were not mere cuts but grave injuries. They knew that the wounded Nagas couldn't be saved.

As the seconds seemed to stretch into hours, the sound of the repaired cannons joined the symphony of war. *BOOM!* The ground shook as the explosives found their marks, sending clods of earth and smoke into the air, adding to the already thick haze that enveloped the battlefield.

With every passing moment, the situation grew increasingly dire for the Nagas. Even Ajaa, with his unparalleled combat skills, could sense the looming shadow of defeat. For every horseman they downed, it felt like two more took their place. The relentless waves of Sardar Khan's cavalry, accompanied by the haunting and ceaseless booming of the cannons, painted a grim picture.

From his vantage point, Vedant could see the Naga sadhus, their once resolute formation now scattered and crumbling beneath the weight of Sardar Khan's cavalry. Each valiant strike by the Nagas was met with two, three, even four counter-strikes. The sacred protectors of Gokul were on the brink of being swallowed whole by the sea of galloping horses. Sardar Khan knew that in retaliation for all that he lost in the last two days, he was about to take the lives of all the Nagas. The gleam of victory was evident in his eyes.

Krishna, eyes filled with concern, begged Vedant once more, 'My Lord, if we don't intervene now, we might be witnessing the last stand of the Naga sadhus. Their bravery is unparalleled, but they are outnumbered and exhausted.'

Vedant's gaze was unwavering, the weight of the decision pressing heavily on his young shoulders. Just as he seemed about to yield to his commander-in-chief's plea, the scene on the horizon changed. Every weapon came to a halt as the charging cavalry and the dying Nagas felt the trembling beneath their feet. Every thought paused as Sardar Khan and Vedant witnessed a cloud of dust rising. Eyes from all directions turned towards the cloud of dust rapidly approaching towards the battleground and from it, an almost mythical figure emerged: a figure of a Naga sadhu, holding a trident, riding on an awe-inspiring, massive bull.

The sight was nothing short of divine. The bull, with its hulking stature, glistening white hide and fierce eyes, bore an uncanny resemblance to Lord Shiva's trusted steed, Nandi. It was as if the scriptures had come alive, with Nandi reincarnated, leading a charge on the earthly plane. The bull's large horns, shaped like crescent moons, gleamed in the sunlight. The pounding of its hooves created a rhythm that sounded like the ancient drums of war.

The cavalry was terrified, Sardar Khan was awestruck and Ajaa was smiling as all of them together saw Shambhu ji sitting atop the beast with the grace and authority of a god. His body was adorned with sacred ash, his dreadlocks flowed behind him like a river, and he held a long and heavy trishul pointed forward. Every aspect of his bearing screamed defiance and determination.

Behind Shambhu ji, ten more Naga sadhus rode forth, each on their own majestic bull that resembled Shambhu ji's steed. Together, they looked like not one but many Lord Shivas holding trishuls on many Nandis reincarnated all at once, forming a formidable cavalry, a force that looked as if it had been summoned straight from the heavens.

The Mathadhish glanced at Ajaa and realized why Ajaa had said that he expected that help would come at the right time. All the Naga sadhus, panting and exhausted, got a breather due to the unexpected heroic appearance of Shambhu ji and the bulls.

It was now eleven bulls and Shiva devotees against more than a hundred horses and horsemen. The embarrassment of calling Shambhu ji a coward and a traitor in the past was evident in Narayan's eyes. This was turning out to be a battle like never before. Mujib, the commander who once sat on Nandi and mocked the devotees and then destroyed the Shiva linga at Kashi remembered what the old priest had warned him, 'Pray to your Gods, for I am sure that one day, riding on his Nandi, Lord Shiva will come to remind you of this night.' The priest's word had come true—the ground beneath him trembled with the weight of old Naga sadhus and their bulls. Unfortunately for Mujib, he was among the first to face the wrath of the bull riders. He was first tossed by Shambhu ji's bull, then stampeded by a few other bulls before the last one in the herd stabbed both its horns in Mujib's stomach and held him high making him a live example for the others to see what would happen if any soldier comes in their way.

Vedant and his commander-in-chief exchanged glances, Vedant's expression a mix of awe and relief. With the hint of a smile, he uttered, 'We wait just a while longer.'

For a moment, the entirety of the battlefield seemed to freeze, all eyes on these unexpected reinforcements. Their approach caused even the seasoned Sardar Khan's cavalry to falter, sensing a new and divine threat.

The blunt contrast between the horses and the bulls was intense. Horses, nimble and agile, had always been the prized warriors in battles, but against the might of these bulls, they looked almost fragile. The horses' eyes widened in fear, their nostrils flaring as they sensed the raw, primitive power of the beasts.

The bulls, powerful and relentless, seemed to feed off the fear of the horses and their riders. Amid the chaos, the horses panicked, scattering in all directions, their riders struggling to control them. The soldiers on foot tried desperately to fend off these new foes, but to no avail.

They moved forward with an unstoppable force. As the bulls charged, horsemen were thrown off their mounts, chaos erupting in the once coordinated ranks. Their sharp horns, like spears gifted by nature, became the bane of the attacking army, piercing shields, armour and all that stood in their way.

The strength of the bulls pushed back the tide of the enemy.

Ajaa, the Mathadhish, Adhiraj and Narayan, upon seeing this turning tide, found a surge of hope within them. Their tired and battered bodies felt re-energized, and they fought with renewed vigour. Their cheers of joy and shouts of encouragement rang across the field.

Sardar Khan's face was a sight to behold as his horses and riders reduced from the hundreds to dozens. Sardar's army, bruised and battered, started retreating. Yet, the battle was far from over. The Afghans, numbering in the hundreds, played their part against the handful of bulls and their riders. The bulls were attacked from all sides with all weapons. The horsemen used their spears, the archers targeted them with arrows and the foot soldiers cut them like butchers with their swords. It was not only the Afghan horsemen and soldiers who were falling—the old Nagas and the young bulls were also among the fallen. Within an hour of their game-changing entry, the Afghan cavalry was completely destroyed before Shambhu ji's last bull collapsed on the field. Shambhu ji gathered his remaining strength to regroup with the remaining Nagas. Ajaa, the Mathadhish, Adhiraj, Narayan and a few more welcomed him with open arms. The total numbers of Nagas standing, including Shambhu ji, was reduced from sixty-three to twenty-seven warriors. Even with the surprising intervention of the old Nagas on bulls, the numbers were against them. Four operational cannons, protected by guards, and the camel cavalry was still unharmed. Hundreds of foot soldiers scattered, regrouped and launched counter-attacks. Arrows rained down, swords clashed and the air was thick with the scent of metal and blood. A hundred camels marched forward, protecting the remaining cannons. Twenty-seven Nagas, tired and panting, were ready to face death, but not to accept defeat.

Krishna's eyes were focused on the brave Naga sadhus, his admiration evident . Turning to his king he spoke, 'My lord, if ever there was a time to join the fray and aid the Nagas, it is now. We could turn the tide!'

King Vedant squinted, gauging the expanse between the two forces. 'Sardar Khan's army is still formidable in size, Senapati. While I admire the spirit of the Nagas, we must think strategically.'

'But, Maharaja sahib,' he argued, passion rising in his voice, 'look at them! They are no soldiers and they have no empire to defend. This is no more just a matter of land and treasure. It has become a war for honour and dharma! We can't simply watch as these brave souls lay down their lives!'

King Vedant, though young and sometimes impulsive, was also astute. 'I've seen the might of these Nagas. I want to see the damage these twenty-seven can do. If they can further diminish Sardar Khan's forces, we will have a better chance of victory with fewer casualties on our end.'

Krishna looked visibly distressed. 'This is unfair.'

King Vedant snapped. 'No! This is war! Risking the lives of our men recklessly is unfair. We will enter the clash at the opportune moment.'

Although Krishna disagreed, he knew there was no point in arguing further. The young king's word was final. All he could do was watch, hoping that the Naga sadhus could stand their ground long enough for Vedant to make his move. 'May Vishnu be on their side!' he murmured in distress.

King Vedant heard this and with a smile said, 'But they are Shiva devotees.'

That was the limit for Krishna, He snapped back, 'Lord Vishnu never turned his back on Shiva and neither will this Vishnu devotee, Vedant!' The statement came as a shock to the young king. His commander- in-chief had just addressed him by his name.

Krishna got down from his horse, ordered the second-in-command to take charge and said, 'I command you to lead this army with utmost loyalty towards the land and its people and protect the king with your life as he is your lord from now till the end of your death . . . or his.'

Agitated, Vedant screamed in anger, 'Who are you to speak about lords and gods? You just betrayed me. I shall behead you for treason.'

'No, Vedant! I did not betray you. I took an oath to my king, your father, and not you. The shackles of my oath

were burnt in the last rites of your father long back and I
have been free since. It was my love for the land and my
king's son that I stood firm as long as I could. My heart bled
when you betrayed King Manohar and I am incapable of
shouldering yet another burden of silence while these Shiva
devotees fight your battle. You wish to kill me? Sure, son!
I am ready to die. That is why I am ready to walk down
this hill where death is certain. But know that I will not go
down before taking at least thirty men. I give you one last
chance to make the right choice. Who do you want those
thirty men to be? Sardar Khan's or yours?'

Vedant looked at his new commander, who had hung
his head. That was enough for Vedant to understand that if
he ordered his soldiers to move against Krishna, he would be
disobeyed again by his new commander and that he must let
Krishna go, or it would lead to revolt among his own troops.

Krishna smiled and spoke again, 'I have to show my
face to my lord, your father, and my god, Shri Vishnu,
both, after my death. Son! Your father was a good king and
I was honoured to serve him. I owe this to him. Give your
new commander a reason to say the same to your son when
you die. May my Vishnu be with you too.'

The brave old man shed the armour bearing the symbol
of Haripur and walked with pride and the courage of
righteousness to perform his duty towards his dharma.

As Hari slowly started walking down the hill, he chanted
'हरि ओम् तत् सत् !' The Vishnu worshipper was going to fight to
the death for the Shiva devotees.

'What is 'हरि ओम् तत् सत्'? asked Thomas .

'In our ancient Hindu scriptures, the world is represented by the mantra "Hari", which means Lord Vishu, the protector of the worlds and one of the Trimurti, which also includes Lord Shiva, the destroyer, and Lord Brahma, the creator. "Om" is the invisible and uncreated aspect of the absolute. "Hari Om Tat Sat" means "that is the truth". That what you and I see with our eyes and that which is beyond our eyes are both the same.' The hiker was in awe as the nameless Naga continued the untold tale.

The Mathadhish, Ajaa, Shambhu ji, Narayan, Adhiraj and all the other remaining naga sadhus were ready to face their fate and Krishna was running to stand with them. The camel cavalry advanced and the cannons continued to drum. Sardar Khan was waiting for the handful remaining Nagas to fall and as King Vedant continued to watch from afar, a strange, surreal rhythm began to vibrate in the air, demanding immediate attention. It started as a low rumble, then intensified into a series of powerful, thunderous thuds that reverberated throughout the very bones of the land. The cacophonous symphony sounded almost like the heartbeat of the earth had been amplified. 'What is generating this vibration?' everyone wondered. Even Ajaa was not expecting any more surprises.

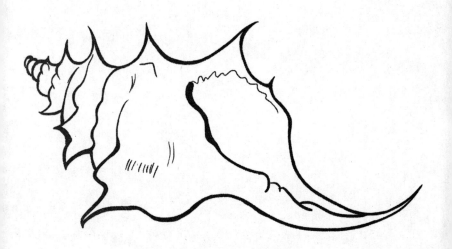

18

Ganesha and Vasuki

'What was that pounding that left everybody confused?' asked the hiker, Thomas, in suspense and totally engrossed in the true tale of sacrifice and brotherhood. The Naga looked at the hiker, smiled and replied,

On the horizon, an awe-inspiring spectacle unfolded. Majestic creatures, their colossal frames glistening under the sun, moved in harmonious synchrony. The elephants, nine of them, their ivory tusks gleaming and trunks swinging gracefully, presented a sight so magnificent, yet so out of place, it felt dream-like.

Each heavy footfall created little dust storms, while their trumpeting calls added a layer of wild music to the air. The Naga sadhus turned their heads, trying to make sense of this bewildering display.

Accompanying the splendour was chaos. Birds, startled, flew off their perches, rising in frenzied flocks. The sight seemed to blur the line between dreams and reality. At the forefront was Vanraaj, sitting atop Dulari, bags hung on her back as before. She was accompanied by a mammoth elephant so large that his size alone sent shivers down the spines of those who beheld him. Behind them, seven gigantic elephants followed in tow, and the baby elephant Golu, though tiny in comparison, ran spiritedly with the group.

To the Naga sadhus, this entrance was not just military reinforcement but divine intervention. The imagery was unmistakable: Vanraaj, with his regal stature and commanding presence, and Dulari, with her massive form and youthful energy, trunk raised and ears flapping, were the image of Lord Ganesha.

'You mean Lord Shiva's son, Lord Ganesha, the elephant-headed god?' asked Thomas. 'Yes, Lord Ganesha, the one who is venerated as the remover of obstacles and the guardian of intellect, who bestows his blessings for success on new beginnings in every significant journey of life,' replied the nameless Naga, and continued.

The closer the elephants got, the more their sheer size became evident. Each massive foot was equivalent to the combined size of five men, and as their feet pounded the ground, they caused it to quake with each step.

The soldiers on the battlefield paused, some in awe, others in sheer terror. These weren't just elephants; they were mountains on the move. They entered the battle field, creating a formidable barrier between the Naga sadhus and Sardar Khan's reorganized army. Sardar Khan's soldiers, caught off guard, momentarily faltered in their reorganization. The camels, not used to such massive creatures, grew restless, their eyes wide with uncertainty. The men operating the cannons hesitated, unsure of where to set their target next.

Ajaa locked eyes with Vanraaj.

'What have you done?' Ajaa's eyes asked Vanraaj, without speaking, brimming with concern.

Vanraaj's response was a wide smile, his eyes twinkling with mischief and resolve, as if saying, 'How could I possibly stand aside?' Adhiraj and all the other Naga sadhus were witnessing all of this from a distance.

Vanraaj's entrance surprised everyone on both sides. The earlier agreement between Ajaa and Vanraaj, where he had asked Vanraaj to leave, seemed a lifetime ago. Without uttering a word, Ajaa gave a nod, a silent acknowledgement of gratitude and newfound respect, accepting his help. Beside him, Narayan, who had always been suspicious of Vanraaj, looked equally humbled. The realization of his previous misjudgement weighed heavily on him.

'Vanraaj, overwhelmed by emotions, after finally finding respect in Narayan's eyes and the nod of acceptance from Ajaa, charged headlong at the enemies without waiting for Ajaa's orders. The sound of his voice ordering his elephants to charge rose above the yelling and screaming of the battlefield. Vanraaj's command seemed to shake the very foundations, the rules and strategies, of war. Ajaa, watching from a distance, recognized the recklessness in Vanraaj's approach. The seasoned warrior could tell that Vanraaj had the heart of a lion but not the training of a soldier.

'Vanraaj! No!' Ajaa's shout was desperate, but it was swallowed up by the cacophony of the battlefield.

One by one, the massive creatures set forth with unparalleled determination. Two elephants charged straight at the active cannons, seeing them as challengers due to their height and the trunk-like shape of the barrels. The soldiers guarding them looked helpless to defend their ground and the cannons. Sardar Khan also helplessly saw these giants play with the cannons like kids with toys. The cannons, which had once seemed like the ultimate weapons, lay in ruins, crushed to irrelevance by the sheer might of these behemoths. Soldiers, previously organized in tight formations, found themselves scattered, trampled and thrown aside by the advancing elephants. The steely discipline of Sardar's troops dissolved into chaos. Spears and arrows, which might have been somewhat effective against a single elephant like Dulari, proved ineffective against a herd of enraged giants. The remaining horses and camels, sensing the tidal wave of danger, panicked and bolted in every direction, adding to the disarray. Sardar Khan's commander-in-chief, Zafar, decided to handle the situation by leading the last line of men standing behind him.

Krishna, the former commander-in-chief of King Vedant, then came and stood with Ajaa and Shambhu ji, without even introducing himself or seeking for permission.

Sardar's once mighty army now appeared on the verge of defeat. The tables had turned, and the tide of the battle had shifted as the elephants had redefined the meaning of dominance on this battlefield.

The bond between Vanraaj and Dulari was evident as Dulari responded to his every gesture and command. The mammoth beasts, following Dulari, thundered towards the formation of the Afghan soldiers. Their charge was unstoppable and fierce.

Sardar Khan's formation comprised of three solid detachments. The central one, sturdy and fierce, was Dulari's target. As she charged, the mysterious large bags on both her sides swayed with each step. Vanraaj held a thin white rope connected to these bags hung at Dulari's sides. Throughout, his grip remained steadfast and his faith in the rope unyielding. Everyone looking at Vanraaj wondered why he held the rope.

Under the Afghan commander-in-chief's leadership, arrow after arrow pierced the air, seeking the elephants as their target. While many missed, enough found their mark, wounding the majestic creatures but the elephant's momentum didn't falter. These attacks only angered the elephants more. With each step, the weight of impending doom became more palpable for the soldiers in their path.

As the elephants thundered into the formation, soldiers, unprepared for such a massive force, desperately lunged at them with their spears. Each thrust, each hit, further hurt the elephants, but they persisted, their large feet causing devastation with every step. Dulari and the herd were not only attacking the soldiers but also defending Golu, their little one, keeping him safe in the middle of their formation, away from all arrows, spears and the cruelty of the Afghans. Golu, with his little feet and trunk, was afraid and in pain seeing his mother Dulari and other elephants struck by arrows with every step forward towards certain death.

Finally, the beasts were in the middle of the soldiers, surrounded, as Abhimanyu had been among the Kauravas. It was their last stand. One by one the elephants were felled, but not before each had broken the bones of men in uncountable numbers.

Amid all this, Golu got his feet trapped under an elephant that fell right beside him, while trying to defend him. Immediately, a few other elephants came close and surrounded Golu. They did not move from this position, forming a perimeter around Golu to keep him safe and hidden. In no time, Golu was secured and enveloped by five fallen elephants, hidden totally beneath them, yet still able to watch his mother and Vanraaj fighting bravely, through the gaps between the elephants gasping for their last breaths.

Vulnerable and surrounded, Vanraaj's fate seemed sealed as blades swung toward him, cutting into his flesh. Within a few seconds, an arrow shot by the commander-in-chief came flying and hit Vanraaj, piercing his ribcage and puncturing his internal organs. Both Vanraaj and Dulari were now bleeding profusely.

'Let's enjoy watching how this last elephant and its rider run away, trying to save their lives,' said the commander-in-chief with a smirk, while all the other Nagas were fighting their own battles.

Losing consciousness slowly, Vanraaj's eyes ran through the enemy's army and stopped at the centre of their formation. Sitting on Dulari's back, his favourite place since childhood, Vanraaj laid his body on her head between both her ears, still holding the thin rope. Tired and powerless, Vanraaj said in a murmur that contradicted his jovial demeanour, 'Dulari, you know where to go now!'

Dulari turned and saw that her family had secured Golu's life with their deaths. She saw her child's eyes from between the bodies of her dead fellows and cried a lone tear before her final move.

She ran towards the centre of the last formation, the biggest of Sardar Khan's reserve army, led by his commander-in-chief. Both Dulari and Vanraaj suffered innumerable blows, bleeding profusely. Fighting the Afghan soldiers around them, Ajaa, Shambhu ji and the Mathadhish watched Vanraaj and Dulari helplessly. Only Narayan could manage to run on with his gadaa, smashing and cutting down every soldier between Vanraaj and him.

Bleeding from every body part, Dulari and Vanraaj reached the centre before Narayan could reach them. Dulari fell, injured, and Vanraaj lost consciousness due to excessive blood loss from his wounds. Seeing Dulari stationary with pain and Vanraaj limp, as if dead, but still holding the rope connected to the bags hung on Dulari, the army of Afghan soldiers walked closer. Dulari lay still, unable to move, looking at the enemies closing in, surrounding Vanraaj and her like hyenas. She kept trying to keep them away from the unconscious Vanraaj by waving her trunk till three soldiers held her trunk firmly and a fourth Afghan cut it clean off, detaching it completely from her face. Her last helpless struggle to free her trunk and her scream brought Vanraaj back to consciousness, while Dulari died in agonizing pain with her trunk totally detached from her body.

Surrounding Dulari and Vanraaj in large numbers, the soldiers thought that Vanraaj was defenceless after Dulari's death, but that was when Vanraaj performed his final trick. Suddenly, he pulled the knots of the sacks on Dulari's back and they came undone. For a moment, there was confusion, a collective intake of breath from both sides. From Dulari's back erupted a flood of serpents, slithering rapidly in every conceivable direction. After Nandi and Ganesha's presence in the war, it was now Vasuki participating, it seemed.

'Vasuki?' asked Thomas, confused. 'The snake you see in my Shiva's neck is Vasuki,' replied the nameless Naga proudly.

'The same snake that Lord Vishnu lay upon?'

'No! That's Sheshnaag! At the end of all four yugas and before the start of the next cycle of the same comes *pralay*—a Sanskrit word that means the period of dissolution or destruction of the manifested universe—according to Hindu philosophy, the end of the world, as you might have heard it described. After pralay, whatever remains is carried forward to the next cycle of yugas. Shesh in Hindi means remaining and Naag means snake. Sheshnaag is the snake that remains even after the holocaust or the end of the world and is carried forward to the next one. Sheshnaag is a serpent demigod, the king of all serpents, who is in service to Lord Vishnu at all times. Ancient Hindu scriptures say that Sheshnaag holds all the planets of the universe on his multiple hoods and constantly sings Vishnu Puranas in praise of Lord Vishnu from all his mouths. He is sometimes referred to as Anant Shesh, which means endless Shesh. It is said that when Shesha uncoils, time moves forward and creation takes place; when he coils back, the universe ceases to exist.

'Lord Vishnu is often depicted as resting on Shesha, accompanied by his consort, Goddess Lakshmi. Shesha never leaves Lord Vishnu's side and is said to have descended upon earth in human incarnations as Lakshman, brother of Vishnu's incarnation Ram, during the Treta Yuga, and as Balrama, brother of Vishnu's incarnation Krishna, during the Dwapar Yuga.'

Right then, another young Naga sadhu walked into the cave with more wood and some food to eat. Thomas was surprised.

'Do not be afraid. He is my disciple,' said the narrator before the hiker could ask. The disciple came forward, greeted the nameless Naga and went out of the cave. and sat outside in the snow.

'It's freezing outside; why is he sitting there?' asked the hiker, concerned.

'That's what he does,' replied the nameless Naga with a smile, looking at his disciple.

'I will ask you later about the origin of Vasuki and Sheshnaag and what the yugas are, but for now, I have to know about Ajaa and the remaining Nagas against Sardar Khan and the other Afghans,' said Thomas, curious like a child, and so the nameless Naga continued.

The bags behind Dulari were loosened by Vanraaj and the movement of all the snakes was like water bursting from a dam, flowing unstoppably, consuming everything before it. Their hissing filled the air, an eerie soundtrack to the devastation they brought. The snakes, each with deadly intent, struck swiftly. Panic ensued as many met their end through the venomous bite of the serpents.

At the death of Dulari and all the other elephants, the battlefield fell silent for a brief moment in the middle of the chaos, honouring the sacrifice of this unexpected warrior.

Narayan rushed to Vanraaj's aid with his mace, killing many Afghan soldiers in his path. But when he finally reached Vanraaj, his heart sank.

Soaked with blood and gasping for breath, Vanraaj looked up at Narayan, his eyes filled with pain. Vanraaj managed a weak smile. 'You refused to let me join you in Gokul. With your permission, can I come with you on your next journey, if you can trust me now?'

Tears welled up in Narayan's eyes. 'Yes! I will take you with me on my next journey. I promise. I trust you with my life, brother!' Narayan leaned down, gently placing his hand on Vanraaj's forehead. 'May my Shiva guide you to eternal peace.'

Just when Vanraaj had bid his last goodbye, a sword swung from behind Narayan. Narayan's severed head tumbled to the battlefield. The man who beheaded Narayan was Sardar Khan himself, his armour and blade stained with the blood of a Naga for the first time.

From a distance, atop a hill, Vedant and his new commander-in-chief watched the scene unfold.

Sardar Khan held Narayan's head aloft, taunting Ajaa and the remaining handful of Nagas, who had been reduced to less than ten with Narayan's death, bleeding and panting, standing against a hundred of the last Afghan soldiers, including the commander-in-chief, Zafar with Sardar Khan himself commanding them all.

Krishna was bleeding from his stomach, Shambhu ji from his chest, Ajaa from his feet and shoulder and the Mathadhish from his head. Seeing the reduced numbers of the Nagas, injured and exhausted, Sardar Khan laughed like a demon and his voice echoed all over the land, the soil damp with the blood flowing from the dead bodies. His laugh was less a cheer and more an announcement of his victory.

'I have more fingers than your numbers now.' And he counted, laughing, '1,2,3,4,5,6,7' but as he finished his counting, a female voice echoed across the plains and the mountains, continuing the count after 7: '8,9,10,11,12, 13,14,15,16,17,18.'

Sardar Khan stopped laughing to look for the source of the voice. The voice was coming from behind Ajaa and the remaining Nagas. Sardar Khan saw Goddess Kaali as if in the flesh. Shyama and Adyama along with two more sadhvis joined Ajaa, their hair open, faces painted in black, holding khadgas in their hands. Along with the sadhvis were all the gravely injured Nagas, two of them crawling on the ground without legs. All of them were dressed in Bhagva.

They were laughing at Sardar Khan louder than Sardar laughed at Ajaa and the remaining sadhus. With their wide open eyes, holding weapons, they took out their long tongues as if teasing and mocking his manhood. This shattered the morale of all the remaining Afghan soldiers. All the sadhvis stopped laughing after a while and Shyama, the bald sadhvi, the senior most of them spoke, 'We can never be covered by your fist, you ignorant fool. You were in the thousands and have been reduced to the hundreds by my 111 warriors, and here we are, still standing.' And then she laughed again. She laughed and with her laughed Shambhu ji, the Mathadhish, Adhiraj, Ajaa and all the other standing and crawling Nagas, shattering the morale of the remaining Afghan soldiers, proving that the Naga warriors were really as invincible as immortals. They laughed in Sardar Khan's face as if the Naga warriors were really indestructible. They laughed as if mocking the stupidity and ignorance of the Afghan commanders, and Sardar Khan's silence was like an acceptance of the Nagas' superiority.

Defeat was evident on the face of Sardar Khan and adding to his dismay was the laughter of the devotees of Kaali and Shiva, affirming it again and again.

King Vedant's new commander-in-chief insisted, 'My king! The battlefield is ripe for our taking, with Sardar's remaining men in disarray.'

Vedant seemed convinced and was about to order the attack, but just before he ordered his forces to charge at the remaining hundred Afghan men, the silhouette of

Jugal Kishore and his brigade of thousands appeared on the horizon.

Depressed and silent, Sardar Khan, furious at his defeat, heard the sound of horses and men and turned. He saw the thousands-strong reinforcement brought by Jugal Kishore standing behind him. He laughed again and with him laughed every remaining Afghan commander and soldier.

He laughed at Ajaa again and said, 'You thought you killed thousands and saved Gokul! We never end. We are born in the thousands every day. Look behind me! There are thousands more for me to expend, but I would rather use them to kill more of you elsewhere.' Vedant's face twisted in frustration. 'Maybe today is not the day for Sardar Khan's death,' he muttered, his resolve faltering.

The new commander-in-chief looked uncertain and asked, 'Should we or should we not join the battle?'

'It's too late,' Vedant sighed, his voice dripping with resignation. 'The Nagas will lose. We cannot risk it.'

And with that, the chance for a united front crumbled, leaving the Nagas to face their destiny alone.

Ajaa looked at the massive size of Sardar Khan's newly arrived army and tightened his fists on both his weapons, the trishul and the gadaa. Before he spoke, he looked at the sadhvis, who looked like Goddess Kaali themselves, the Mathadhish, with the wisdom of age, Adhiraj with his shankh and the other injured Nagas still standing steady, ready for their orders, ready to face whatever came next. Then he looked at Krishna who stood against his own king to fight for the Nagas against the Afghans and finally, he looked at Shambhu ji, standing with his axe. Ajaa was still unaware of the fact that Shambhu ji's real name was King Dhyanendra and King Dhyanendra was none other than the answer to the question he kept asking his deaf and dumb past—King Dhyanendra, the man bound by a promise who could not say, 'Ajaa! My son! You are a prince and I, King Dhyanendra, your father.'

The Mathadhish, looking at both of them, felt his guilt rise in him, and Adhiraj watched all of it with no authority to speak among them. Finally, Ajaa spoke, 'I can speak a thousand words to motivate you all, but you are no less than me and do not require motivation. Some of you have lived more years than me, the others have older and wiser souls than mine, the remaining are women, who lay the foundation of the world and the earth we live in. The only words I wish to share with you are that we are alive and so . . . it's not over yet.'

Each one of the eighteen remaining Nagas prepared themselves, tightened their fists and wiped their blood and sweat. The Mathadhish and Shambhu wiped their tears too, along with their blood and sweat.

Together they roared, 'Har Har Mahadev!'

The handful remaining of Sardar Khan's army, the thousands under Jugal Kishore, Vedant and the gods watched it all—the Nagas holding their ground, ready to kill and die in the war that was never spoken about in history of Bharat. Everything on the battle ground seemed to have come to a halt but there was somebody in the north moving unstoppably, ready to kill and prepared to die. Dhruv was approaching the snow-covered mountains in search of the ocean of Nagas living in the freezing snow, unaware of how hot the flowing blood on the land had become.

'What happened next? What happened to Ajaa? Did he learn that his father fought alongside him?' asked Thomas, who was still weak but was adamant to know more about the war.

'Enough for the day! You need to rest. Drink this and you will recover by tomorrow,' replied the nameless Naga, offering Thomas soup in an old copper bowl.

Thomas had begun to trust the nameless Naga and so he accepted the bowl gratefully and started sipping the soup.

'You will feel dizzy and sleepy after this drink. Do not be afraid, confused or suspicious. Had I intended to kill you, you would have been dead long ago. So sleep well and you will see a good morning tomorrow,' replied the nameless Naga.

By the time Thomas heard that, he was already dizzy and sleepy.

The Naga disciple walked in and set up a temporary bed for his comfort.

Sipping the soup, Thomas asked, 'How do you know all this about an incident 650 years old that is not chronicled anywhere? What's your name?'

'I am a nameless Hindu. My name does not matter. No more questions for the day. Now sleep.'

In no time, Thomas dozed off.

Thomas spent the night beside the fire in that cave, but the questions continued in his head until he woke up.

The next morning, Thomas opened his eyes with the morning light and felt much more energetic and physically strong. He stood on his feet for the first time since he had met the nameless Hindu Naga. He looked around but found no traces of the one who had saved him.

Instead, there was something lying on the ground where the nameless Hindu was sitting. Thomas walked closer to see what it was.

It was a shankh used as a paperweight that seemed centuries old. Underneath the shankh was the hidden book of the Hindu Naga who had no name. Thomas opened the first page of the book and found a one-line note with a map that read,

'This map will help you find your way back to civilization.'

With several unanswered questions about the eighteen remaining Naga sadhus and sadhvis against the hundreds of Afghans, backed by a reinforcement of thousands more, and Vedant standing helpless, Thomas picked up the shankh, the map and the book and walked out of the cave, looking for the nameless Naga.

Somewhere deep in the snowy mountains, walking behind the Hindu sage, the disciple asked, 'What happened to those eighteen Naga sadhus and sadhvis?'

To be continued . . .

Acknowledgements

Mumbai is a sea of stars but one that shone the brightest in my eyes lives in Delhi. I wanted to meet him, sit in front of him, watch him work and see his life up close. I just wanted to be around him and absorb his aura and presence. It was bordering on obsession when I got a chance to finally meet him and tell him that a face and name like mine also exists in the crowd of lakhs of his fans, admirers and lovers. I never knew what it meant to be starstruck until the day he looked at me.

It is said that if you are a fan of any star, never meet them because you will be disappointed. The aforementioned saying is wrong as his reality matched my imagination of him. Now, he knows that I won't wait for Diwali and his birthdays to wish and pray for his health and prosperity. Saurabh Dwivedi (Bhaiya), thank you for simply being who you are and thanks to the lady behind you. Gunjan Sangwan (Bhabhi), I bow down to you for the light and warmth in my brightest star.

Some things are beyond comprehension in one lifetime, so souls come back to understand the unsolved. I believe in reincarnations and past-life connections. Something very pious and godly was incomplete between them and me in our past lives, and that's why I met them in this life again. A family that is full of love and unity, care and blessings. A family that does not permit the emotions to fade away due to distance. A family that can feel your pain and reduce it with their selfless hugs, with no expectations in return. A family that can genuinely accept you as one of their own with no judgement and feel proud of your achievements as if it's their personal victory. Rosy Mehta (my love), S.K. Mehta (Rosy's love), Sandeep Bedi (brother) and dearest Jyotika Bedi. I am still trying to understand my past-life connection and the bond—which was instant—with you all. I pray to my Shiva and my Vishnu that the mystery of our past lives connection remains unsolved till eternity so that the incompleteness of our karmic circle continues for all my future reincarnations and that I keep meeting you all in every lifetime. You all have healed me in some unexplainable way and beautified my soul for the rest of the world to see. I can write 100 pages on our two breakfast meetings, but I will leave the ninety-nine pages empty for 100 or more meetings with you all in this lifetime.

I love you all more than my heart can contain, and at this very moment, while I am typing this out, trying to show you all your place in my heart, I am crying. I am overwhelmed because I am a part of all of you and you are a part of me. Thank you for accepting a nobody like me with your open arms and absorbing me selflessly. I owe you all and I don't wish to repay and close the accounts.

In debt of your love . . .

Yours,

Debtor forever

I was bragging about my devotion and admiration for a man, denoting him as my Ram instead of saying his name and a girl I hardly knew, was patiently listening to it all. I continued paying my respect and love towards my Ram and this girl with a consistent smile kept listening. But her smile was not because of the devotee but for the idol. After she had had enough of me and my talks on my Ram, she signalled me to come closer. I bent a little to bring my ears closer to her lips and then she said, 'He may be Ram for you, but for me, he is my Krishna.' Bang!

Thanks to both Ram and Krishna, it was not a debate. Had it been one, I would have happily lost to her on that one statement at the end of my long talk. It was enough for me to understand that she knew more about Ram than I knew about Krishna; I realized, she was closer to Vishnu. I have been speechless before too, but never as happy. 'What did you say, your name was?' I asked. 'Chandrali Mukherjee!' she replied with the same satisfied smile she had on for a while. She knew she had won. Now I knew the reason behind her smile. Now I know a little more than before. Chandrali! Thank you for becoming my little (not so little) sister. May my Ram and Krishna always keep showering their blessings upon us.

You have the art of energizing people around you. You are full of life and light up wherever you go, unbothered about what they think or talk about you. You! Not hesitant to laugh with your whole wide mouth open and walk in your own style and pace, unapologetically. Graceful in your unmasked and unfiltered version too, inviting and welcoming with open arms, Saumya Kulshreshtha, my friend, it's a pleasure knowing you.

Sandeep Leyzell Bhai! Thank you for trusting me on this one. This book has seen the light because of your faith in me, and I will do my best to never break the bond of trust, confidence and belief between us. You are the sweetest and the most genuine film producer I have come across. It is a dream come true for any story developer and screenwriter to get a producer like you. I feel truly blessed, and I promise to keep you in my prayers always.

One of a kind, gentlehearted man who wants nothing in exchange for all that he offers. His suggestions are invaluable and so is he—Manish Pandey, teach me to be you. Your presence itself is a silent assurance that all is well. Thank you for backing me up for no reason. I hope I get a chance one day in this lifetime to do something for you.

Parakh Om Bhatt, it would not have been easy without you to get the Gujarati version of my previous books released. Just wanted to thank you for handling that for me, brother. It will be my pleasure if you do the Gujarati translation of *The Naga Warriors* too. May we keep working for and with each other all our lives.

I was told he is a podcaster and a successful businessman before I met him but he is also a winner of hearts—joyous and loving, sensitive yet strong at heart. He is grateful to everyone around him. Ashutosh Pratihast, lots of blessings. You know that I have your back. I am proud of you.

The rawness in you guys is adorable. The warmth and homely environment you create at your place are so positive and loving. Time flies with you guys. Thank you for considering doing podcasts with me. It has played a big role in shaping my career. The boys behind 'The Real Hit' podcast—Shubham, Deepak and Piyush. Love you guys.

He is not just an astrologer for me. He is a friend; bad at expressing his emotions, good at silently doing his duties and maintaining relations. Arun Pandit, keep taking care of my stars and planetary moments silently. I am grateful to you and your team.

Met them as professionals, felt friendly and became family. They served me food and opportunity and then took care of me when I fell ill in Delhi. Deepali Sharma and Yuvraj Malik, I am indebted to you both, and I hope a window opens soon for us so that I can serve you at my home in Mumbai.

Scan QR code to access the
Penguin Random House India website